SWAMPY JO

Enjoy!

Jennifer Rouse Barbeau

March 21/2016

SWAMPY JO

Novel and Illustrations

by

Jennifer Rouse Barbeau

ScrivenerPress

Library and Archives Canada Cataloguing in Publication

Barbeau, Jennifer Rouse

Swampy Jo / Jennifer Rouse Barbeau.

ISBN 978-1-896350-40-0

I. Title.

PS8635.O8645S83 2010 jC813'.6 C2010-904808-3

Book design: Laurence Steven
Cover design: Jennifer Rouse Barbeau
Interior illustrations: Jennifer Rouse Barbeau
Cover photo of author: Nicolas Barbeau

Published by Scrivener Press
465 Loach's Road,
Sudbury, Ontario, Canada, P3E 2R2
info@yourscrivenerpress.com
www.scrivenerpress.com

We acknowledge the support of the Canada Council for the Arts and the Ontario Arts Council for our publishing program.

ONTARIO ARTS COUNCIL
CONSEIL DES ARTS DE L'ONTARIO

Canada Council for the Arts
Conseil des Arts du Canada

This novel is dedicated to the memory of my mother,
Madeleine Andréa Pilon Rouse

Acknowledgements

Sincere thanks to the many people who helped with *Swampy Jo*: publisher Laurence Steven for invaluable editorial advice; Janet Calcaterra, Laurie Kruk and Catherine Dean for honest feedback; the members of Conspiracy of Three for a venue to share my work; readers Anne Barbeau, Laurie Walinga, Roger and Arlene Barbeau, Lisa Renaud, Shirley Cockburn and Mary Schaefer; Jay Barbeau for support during the first draft; Barry Grills for partnership in all things literary and beyond; and to the many writers, friends and family members who have provided encouragement along the way.

And special thanks to you, the reader, for meeting Swampy Jo. Feel free to reach me at www.jenniferrousebarbeau.com

Prologue

This story is not about me. It is the story of everyone else.

If you walk through the park, sometime, you might see a knot of small, neat graffiti sprayed onto the black rock outcrop by the walkway, or onto the bricks of the retaining wall at the beach. You need to know that it wasn't my idea to put it there, to put my name with his. Only the idiot who painted our names, my name and his together, cannot spell. The inscription reads

SWAMPY JOE
POKETS
(YOFUS).

It's because of the sign of the Mystic Cross that he wanted

to mark it, to remember. The magic of it. The idea of the magic. Some people are over-awed by that.

People like me.

My name is Sarah Joanne Bradley, but everyone calls me Swampy Jo. The nickname came about when I was five years old, the year I lost my father. I am told I lost a fight with a very large mud puddle where our beach used to be. When we had a beach. I am also told that I haven't quite found my way out of that mud puddle yet.

No one minds if my brother Joseph is clean or not. What goes for him should go for me.

"But he is only nine years old," Mom tells me. "You're fourteen."

I don't see how that matters.

Joseph wasn't even a year old when we left our big home on the lake. He had just started to speak. Even as a baby, he was mostly interested in himself. He would slap his chest with his fat little hands, and call himself "Yofus." Everyone still calls him that.

The nicknames stuck: Swampy Jo, Yofus. I guess we're a family that does not like to leave things as they are, or perhaps we don't get things right the first time.

I suppose you need to know about Pockets to understand. But it's important that you know it wasn't my idea to tattoo our names on the hard black stone of a public park on the opposite side of the lake where I tried to drown myself in a huge black mud puddle the day my Daddy left. My Aunt Cassie says: "You don't have to parade your private parts in public." Still, I will tell you what I can, what I must for you to understand. But there are still secrets. As Aunt Cassie says, the only thing more uncomfortable than being caught in a lie is being caught in the truth.

Chapter One

We have lived in a lot of places, Mom, Joseph and I. Nine different places in nine years. Joseph was nine months old when we lost dad and had to leave our big home on the lake. We moved to a geared-to-income apartment building on a hill, with an Olympic-size swimming pool and a fully-loaded games room. Where Mom would feed kids who would otherwise go without supper. Where the Dobermans in the apartment overhead would leak urine from the bottom of their cage right through our living room ceiling, leaving yellow streaks down the jewel-coloured walls.

"The crap shack," Aunt Cassie calls that one.

Then there was the place by the railroad tracks, just opposite the downtown core, with the baseboard heater that kept shorting out. There were other places, more or less the same. We just kept moving, like criminals on the run. Some nameless, unspeakable evil seemed to haunt our every step, reflected in Mom's restlessness, in the triple locks she put on the doors and in her guarded chats with strangers who were never allowed to become friends. Each time we moved, Mom would pack up our things, move them and unpack them. Then she would get down on her knees to scrape the crud off the back of our newest toilet. It was like a form of prayer, or penance perhaps.

I used to wonder what it was she had to confess. I was foolish enough then to want to know.

Once each new toilet was purified, baptized and anointed, Mom would fuss and sort our increasingly threadbare things, and paint the walls a fresh new jewel tone. The whole process would take months and months. In the middle of the night, I'd find Mom asleep in a heap with a putty knife in one hand and a Mr. Clean spray bottle in the other. Her mouth gaping. Her bottom eyelids reaching upward, as if even closing her eyes no longer came naturally.

No matter how hard she worked, she never felt any place was right. And so we'd move again.

Summers meant work at the greenhouse on a barren stretch of highway near the airport, where if you stepped outside the dryness caught in your throat and there was nothing to look at but hard, black rock. But the greenhouse was lush with fruit and vegetables, and potted blooms that were brought in for retail sale from a nearby farm. The work days were long, dawn to dusk and then some. Joseph and I tried to stay out of the way; we always tagged along "to save on daycare." When Mom got tired, she would sit among the rows of marigolds, breaking off the dried heads until the flowers were perfect, row upon row.

For four winters, Mom worked retail in one mall or another, "for not enough money," she said. So, finally, she enrolled in university, which she had never done before.

"You'll never make it, sis," Aunt Cassie clucked. "You quit school at fifteen because it was too much for you. How do you figure you can make it now?"

Aunt Cassie meant no harm, of course—not then, and not now. At fourteen, I still believe that no one ever means any harm.

But I'm starting to wonder.

"It's *all* too much for me, Cass," Mom would explain. "At least this too much has a better job at the end of it."

"Maybe," Aunt Cassie said, not sounding convinced.

Mom didn't take to university very easily. She would sit sometimes for hours, days, staring at an unopened hundred-dollar textbook. It took all her strength to crack the cover. She stayed up late at night, at first just gathering courage, then reading, re-reading, taking long pages of notes. In spite of all that writing, a single sentence for an essay would take hours. Hours. I would find her asleep in the tub at six in the morning, the water cold as ice. Asleep at the kitchen table. Asleep with a bite of sandwich in her mouth.

And all the time we kept moving, always trying to find somewhere less expensive to live. "This is the last time," she would say.

But it never was.

This year we have moved in with Aunt Cassie, into her basement. It would not be accurate to call our place an apartment, because you have to go through my Aunt's kitchen to reach the stairs leading down. Nothing needs cleaning in Aunt Cassie's house. Ever. The toilet does not need scraping, but Mom does it anyway. By now the habit has been programmed into her DNA.

It is a stroke of luck (or punishment, perhaps?) that we have moved here. This is where I will meet Pockets. This is where the veil of lies and truth will start to unravel.

This is where I will start to come undone.

On our first Sunday in early September, an unexpected chill seeps through the basement walls, the kind of chill that only stops when it reaches your marrow. Mom has been awake for hours, has not really slept at all. She has traded a night's sleep for a painted wall that reaches from stairs to kitchen: a lusty berry color, like the filling of a pie. I notice that the more Mom does these days, the slower she moves, to the point where it doesn't seem that she is moving at all. Like Parkinsons' patients who shake so much they become still, Mom gives the illusion of being frozen in place by too much movement. She is a spinning top cranked too tight to ever turn again.

By nine-thirty this morning, Mom has cleaned the paint rollers and brushes, and has stored them neatly away by ten. She fusses over breakfast near eleven, showers at noon, re-wets her hair to blow-dry it at one-thirty. By quarter to three in the afternoon, we are ready to join Aunt Cassie and her daughter Madison—my cousin—for a walk in the park.

"Is unc' coming?" Joseph asks.

Aunt Cassie shakes her head. "He's out of town," she explains.

"Again?"

"Yofus! Manners, please." Mom's voice bounces up from downstairs, to where the rest of us are gathered by the door. "I'll just be a minute, Cass. I can't find my purse."

"You don't need your purse, sis. We're just going to the park. There's nothing to buy, anyway."

"Still," Mom says from below.

"It's just he's gone a lot," Joseph pouts. "Don't ya miss him?"

Aunt Cassie has one hand on the door knob, her eyes on the empty stairwell. "Your uncle and I have found a balance. I do miss him, sometimes, but his job takes him out of town. We see each other a couple of times a week. Maybe it's not for everyone. He takes care of the money, I take care of the rest. Sis, you coming?"

"So he's never around." Joseph hangs his head, sinks his fists into his pockets. "So I'm the only man in the house."

Madison snickers. "Oh this house has a man, alright, Yofus. He just has a long leash, eh Mom?"

Joseph looks at me, as if I know how to make this right. As if I'm the freakin' dog catcher. As if I can slap down some kind of man-dog fine.

Mom's head emerges from the stairwell opening, rising a foot at a time in slow motion. "Do you think I'll need gloves, Cass?" She stops on the top step, catching her wind.

The city's central park is a ten minute walk from Aunt Cassie's, over an ugly metal walk-bridge that spans the railway yard below. Harsh street sounds above and clanging metal underneath, then all at once we've crossed into the muffled maze of the oldest residential neighbourhood in town. Regal homesteads with settled stone driveways and proud iron gates nestle among towering trees, which cling to the earth as a prelude to the vast parkland ahead. A sharp breeze from off the lake, just ahead of us now, rattles the crunchy leaves freeze-dried to their branches by the morning's sudden frost: they jostle crisply in the wind, muttering secrets.

Following the interlocking stone pathway along the water brings us past one sand beach after another, past an elegant gazebo atop a rock outcropping, where I imagine people dancing to live music on a warm summer evening. Past the half dome of the amphitheater, glaring like a huge eyeball cut into the hillside, its concrete seats unwelcome now with their layer of sparkling mist. The park is deliciously quiet.

But not for long.

"Woo-hee!" Madison shrieks. "Look at the nutcase out on the water! Woo-ha! He's gonna freeze his balls off! It's freakin' freezing out here!"

Joseph laughs and laughs. We are not allowed to say 'freakin'.

Madison is not at all like me. For one thing, she is almost six feet tall, and skinny, with long dark hair and a tendency to speak through her nose. She is fifteen and won't wear an ounce of fabric more than necessary against the day's cold. (Aunt Cassie makes all Madison's clothing by hand—even her jeans—from the most current *Vogue* patterns. Her clothes fit like gloves—skin-sticking rubber gloves. And Aunt Cassie gets up early every morning to do Madison's hair. Mom says Aunt Cassie has made a religion out of motherhood.) No one ever calls Madison anything but Madison.

All you need to know about me is that in every way I am what Madison is not.

Today Madison is wrapped in a charcoal fitted fleece jacket over a periwinkle blue Tee and black jeans with just the right amount of fullness at the bottom. Her dark hair is loosely braided down her back, where it bounces with her as she prances and points at the figure on the water.

"Total nutbar, that's what *that* is," Madison snorts. "Windsurfing, and it's practically snowing."

We all look at the dark figure in a black wetsuit and bare feet, slashing the fierceness of waves and sky with the blade of his surfboard.

"What a day to windsurf," Madison hoots. "Hey fruitcake! Got any nuts left?...Hey! That's Pockets! Mom, it's Pockets! Ooh-hoo, look at him!" A lusty chuckle rumbles at the back of Madison's throat. "Damn, he's crazy but he sure looks good."

"He *is* a good looking boy," Aunt Cassie says, more to the wind than to any of us.

"Bugger," Madison sulks. "He'd be a good catch if he wasn't a player."

"What do you mean a player, Madison?" Joseph asks twice, over the wind and Madison's hysterics.

I am thankful he has asked, because I don't know either.

"Oh, Yofus! You're so cute!" she gushes, with more condescension than necessary. "A player is a boy that likes to... *date*..." She says this with wide eyes and a little laugh. "Yes, a boy that likes to date a lot of girls at the same time. Look. He's coming off the water now. I'll just go give him a hand with his board. Woohoo, Pockets! I'm coming, baby! Jeez, Swampy Jo, get the freak out of my way!"

The windsurfer looks at me and laughs. '*Swampy Jo*,' his mouth says.

We are getting closer, and the boy in the wetsuit is still staring me down. I can see from here that his lips are blue, his feet white from the cold. Madison is bouncing around him now, her eyes and hands all over him. He does not seem to notice.

"His name is Paul. Paul Holditch," my Aunt is saying. "Both his parents are lawyers. He lives in that place right over there, on the point. The brown three-storey one with all the windows."

She indicates an ultra-modern stone and glass construction of several stories, wedged between two haughtier homes from another era.

"They say the place is 5,000 square feet. The entire top

floor—see that bank of windows facing the water?—is nothing but master bedroom!" Aunt Cassie pauses wistfully. "He seems like a nice kid," she says with a question in her voice, as though there were some bit of evidence that could reveal otherwise. "He's sixteen years old, in Madison's class. Was held back a grade, I think. Not much of a student, apparently." She laughs. "I'm not sure why they call him Pockets. Always has his hands in his pockets, maybe. Or is loaded down with pockets full of cash. Who knows? You know how it is with nicknames. Right, Swampy Jo?"

He has started up the hill now—Paul, Pockets—with his board in hand, barely listening to Madison chirping beside him. He looks right at me, a bare, hard stare. His dark eyes are impenetrable, reflecting neither earth nor sky, too black to mirror anything. The wind goes through me, snapping at my spine.

"We'd better get back for dinner," Mom says. "I don't want the kids to be tired for their first day in a new school."

Another new school, I think. Fun.

I follow Paul with my eyes, watch how his hips move in a steady, even stride. There is something about him, the curve of his body from shoulder to hip, the ease of it, that makes me want to touch him. The wind picks up his dark hair, restyles it, lets it fall. He is beautiful. He does not look back.

That is when I see my dad.

***

My dad is not dead. It is worse than that. The truth is he kicked our dust off his heels and left us. We see him around town sometimes, by chance. It is like viewing the body of a loved one laid out at a funeral home, coming upon it unexpectedly again and again, without ever being able to bury it.

Mornings are not good for me. For timeless moments I remain stuck in the quicksand of heavy dreams. Unable to move, or think. Or breathe.

My dad. My dad.

The memory of yesterday in the park plays painfully behind my eyelids. He is so well dressed; it is always what I notice first. His face just freshly shaven, regardless of the hour. This time his 'accessory'—his newest girlfriend, that is—wears a short fur jacket, custom made by his store: just the thing for a windy Sunday walk in the park. The raccoon mane snickers at me from the back of her pretty neck. Her perfect blond hair arches in the wind like the sails of a ship.

My dad sees me watching him. He looks away quickly, nods at Aunt Cassie, stares blankly at Mom as though she is someone he should know but can't quite place. Then he falls all to pieces over Joseph. Dad is the only one on the planet who does not call my baby brother 'Yofus.' Dad ruffles his hair, airplanes him around the nearest tree. He introduces his accessory as Marla, or Carla, or something. He never looks at me again. I don't know why he hates me.

I force my eyes to open.

This morning, Mom is asleep on the couch; not lying down, but sitting up with her legs twisted under her, an open textbook propped on her knees. Her back is perfectly straight, but her neck is bent at an awkward angle. If she has been asleep for long, that's going to hurt.

"Mom," I say as gently as I can. "It's ten to eight. We've gotta fly if we're gonna make school. Mom."

I try a gentle shake of her shoulder. Her neck bounces rigidly.

"Mom, come on. Today's our first day of school."

Mom's eyes flicker open. She has to use her hands to help straighten her neck. I am off before she begins to groan.

"Yofus! Get up!" I yell as I pass Joseph's door. "Drag your scrawny butt out of bed, it's late!"

Joseph has his own room. I bunk in with Mom, in a single bed tucked into the corner beside her double one. You would be hard pressed to find evidence of me in that room, however, if you looked. I do not take much space, and I do not leave much of a wake behind me as I go. Except, as Joseph might say, for the massive shadow I cast as I go by. Hilarious.

I make my bed, matching the seams on the bedspread in an even line. Using my peripheral vision, I smooth a few wayward hairs into place, avoiding my reflection. I think of Dracula, whose image cannot appear in a mirror, and wonder: *if you have no reflection, then do you really exist?* I throw on some jeans and fly upstairs before Mom.

In Aunt Cassie's kitchen, Madison is poking at half a grapefruit. She is dressed in mauve from head to toe, which sets off the dark cascade of her hair perfectly. "I could get my eyes done," she is saying, "and my boobs. Teri had her boobs done over the summer."

"Breasts," Aunt Cassie corrects. She is at the sink and does not look up.

"Whatever. It's no wonder she got them done anyway—she was so flat! Well, she's not flat anymore. You should see those things. Big as grapefruit!" The grapefruit on Madison's breakfast plate looks suddenly disgusting to me.

Outside, the cold feels good.

***

Because of the move, I have missed one week of classes. This will be my first day in high school; I am fourteen years old, beginning grade nine. I am here alone to register because Mom (always pressed for time and running behind this morning) has to get Joseph to his new school. She drops me off across the street.

"Don't worry," she says distractedly. "You look fine. Tuck your shirt in... no, maybe not. No big deal. No one will even notice you. Just blend in. Nothing to it."

Then she is off, with Joseph tucked in beside her, munching a peanut butter bagel.

Nothing seems to have been accomplished in the week that I have missed: students still mill about the halls after the bell sounds, peering at the schedules in their hands, obviously perplexed as to where the next class might be. At least I'm not the only one who doesn't know where I should be. I feel invisible and conspicuous at the same time.

In the principal's office, I am given a locker number, but no lock.

"Hang up your jacket, then meet Mr. Habbernashy in his office. Blue door, on the left. Mr. Habbernashy will be your guidance counsellor."

The secretary does not pretend to smile.

My locker is up one flight of stairs. Two very tall boys standing in front of it sense my hesitation and move marginally to one side, one back curving in a familiar, disarming sway. It's Paul, the windsurfer from yesterday's walk on the beach.

He turns his dark-as-death eyes on me. "Name's Swamp-something," he says, waiting for me to fill in the blanks.

"Swampy Jo," I stammer. "Sarah Jo, actually."

"And your brother's Yogourt, or what?" The timbre of his voice moves up my spine: I feel it more than hear it.

"Yofus. From Joseph, um, somehow." I can't think of anything else to say.

Paul looks at me. Long. He cocks his head, and looks some more.

"Pockets! Yo!" the other boy snarls, squinting at Paul, wondering why he should care about this new, dumpy kid.

I escape to the blue door of Mr. Habbernashy's guidance office, feeling a bit like throwing up. The door sports a yellow happy face sticker beneath the name engraved on a brass plate: "Edmund Ernest Habbernashy BSc BA BEd. Guidance Counsellor." Unsure if I should knock, or just enter, I do both.

Mr. Habbernashy is frowning deeply over some papers in a file. He closes it abruptly as I enter. The file cover reads "Sarah Joanne Bradley, Personal and Academic History."

I have never before understood what the expression 'pudding face' meant, but Mr. Habbernashy has to be that, personified. His smile is all pudgy folds and ripples, his pale skin lumpy and pockmarked. His dark eyes are two raisins in a sea of tapioca. The rest of him is perhaps plump or stocky or strong or squishy. It is difficult to tell. He is hideous and harmless all at once.

"So you're—You must be, then: Sarah Joanne?" He speaks in a sloppy way, laughing between words for no reason. A fresh pudding-face smile brims over as if I have made his day.

"Most people," I lie, "call me Sarah Jo."

Mr. Habbernashy thrusts a huge dimpled hand at me. "Sarah Jo it is then. Pleasure to meet you."

I reach out to shake, but fumble the maneuver. I do not keep all my fingers together, so that his eager clasp traps my thumb and forefinger above his grip. My index finger just sticks out on top of his hand, when it should be properly tucked inside.

My face gets hot. I feel like an idiot.

"Well then," he says, quite seriously, looking at my misplaced digit. "Yes, well, that's it then. I can see you're very unique."

He smiles warmly, and mercifully lets my hand go.

"Do you like it here, Sarah Jo?"

I shrug. "I just got here."

"Yes, yes, you just got here." He nods pensively, giving me a long appraising look.

I look at the tweed carpet, at the ceiling tiles—three don't match, they're the wrong shade of white—at the walls, with rows and rows of text books. At the framed diplomas—three of them: one in Science (Psychology), one in Philosophy, one in Education. At the colour-coded cast of a brain on the corner of his desk, which I sincerely hope is made of plastic.

Who is this man?

Mr. Habbernashy's ugly eyes dart from the brain to my face.

"Oh," he spits, "my brain. I'm a philosopher, by education. Well, first I studied …," he waves his hand as though annoyed at his slow brain, "I study, still, psychology, the research side, and philosophies. What really makes people do the things they do. That's what interests me. The why of human behaviour."

His look is piercing.

"By the way," he says importantly: "Habbernashy's the name. Long name, and odd too, hmmm? Just think of 'button seller.' 'Haberdasher' means 'seller of small inconsequential stuff like buttons and thread.' Stuff that seems unimportant, until you try to get along without it. Imagine if your clothes had no buttons or thread! Anyway, that's a haberdasher. Habbernashy is almost the same. Of course, that's an old fashioned word: haberdasher. Perhaps you don't know it?"

He searches my face earnestly.

"I think it might be easier to remember just plain Mr. Habbernashy," I say.

I feel a little like a mouse being toyed with by a very inquisitive pussy cat: a kind of getting-to-know-your-appetizer ballet.

"Mr. H will do, if you like," he smiles. "Most of the kids call me that. Of course, many of them are monosyllabic."

He smirks.

"But you, Sarah Jo, are very smart. Gifted, I think the word is." He taps the heavy file on his desk, the one with my name on it. "They change these words, now and again... A rose, by any other name... But the relevant facts are—Yes. You are smart." A fat finger stabs the fact, as if it were an invisible Pillsbury dough boy on his desk. "You have just moved." Another stab. "And you are Sarah Jo Bradley. Yes. Yes. Yes."

The room is heavy with the silence of this momentous discovery. I dare not breathe.

"Well, time is ticking, isn't it, Sarah Jo? We'd better get you settled into your classes. Well! In grade nine you will follow the same curriculum as everyone else. You'll be in the advanced classes, of course. And you get to choose one elective." He peers at a jumbled chart on the wall. "Luckily, I should be able to get you into the more challenging ones!"

He jabs dough boy with a merry fist in the air.

I fidget. Once you are identified as gifted, no one ever cuts you any slack.

"And for the elective, hmmm?" Mr. H grins like the Cheshire cat. "What interests you, Sarah Jo?"

Perhaps I don't think quickly enough. It isn't his fault. What I want for the single course I can choose is something quiet, something simple. Something I already know how to do. I want to say "Creative writing" or "English literature." I love to read. And write: it is the one time I can get all the words I want to use out quickly enough, the one way my words can be heard, if only in the mind of the teacher who has to grade them.

But I do not speak quickly enough. Mr. H expounds on the gifts of this and that teacher, of the merits of this and that course. He ends exuberantly with

"Now, Miss Trundle's drama class, she's amazing, has won awards throughout . . . ," he blusters and his eyes grow round, ". . . well, everywhere. Yes, Theatre Arts, now there's a challenge for someone quiet like you! Shall we?"

I am not very good at saying no.

He walks me to the door, my hand swallowed by both his thick fists. There is a spot of something gravy-coloured on his lapel. "If you're interested in discovering what interests you, my Sarah Jo, you could come by once a week, at lunch. I've got tests: Personality tests! Myers Briggs tests! All kinds of the most interesting tests!"

He looks at my hair, my ears, my eyes.

"We could find out all about you," he says quietly.

I don't take my hand away from his; I am hardly sure it is my own to take. I wait for him to let me go.

"Thank you," I say, because it is what I always say.

***

Miss Trundle's drama class is in full swing by the time I find her classroom. Identified as a 'drama studio' on the handwritten schedule in my hand, this space is as boxy and colourless as the other classrooms I've passed, although the floor is carpeted and multi-tiered, like a lecture hall without seats. In fact, there are no chairs or desks anywhere. Students are on their feet in ragged groups, blowing air through their flapping lips.

"Let the sound and energy move through you," Miss Trundle urges, waving her freckled arms. Flags of freckled skin quiver in response. "Think: loose, loose, I'm loose as a goose."

My new classmates shake their heads and hands, babbling freely, unaware that I've joined them. They are all sizes: stocky, tall, bulky, wiry. Yet they all look at ease. They maintain eye contact with each other, communicating confidence while they rattle their jowls and make motor-boat sounds. They look like exotic birds performing extravagant courting dances in the wild.

"Now peep, class. Peep-peep-peep," Miss Trundle sings, "in high voices, yes, just like that. Peep-peep-peep. Now deep. Deep peeps. Peeeep. Peeeep. Feel the sound move in your chest. Breathe through the diaphragm. Deep, deep, purple peeps."

Miss Trundle clutches her ribcage with her brown-freckled hands. "Feeeel your diaphragm move in and out, under your ribcage. Peep. Peep. Peep. Now move." Miss Trundle begins to lumber across the middle platform, peeping from under heavy, faded-red bangs.

My classmates, male and female, in sneakers and heels (one barefoot, in pyjama pants), move in exaggerated strides, some low and elongated, others bouncy or dragging. "Be anything, anyone. Be loose and free. Your only job is to be."

Thirty-or-so students flit about, acting out, all in their own way, engaging with each other through eye contact and facial expression, through synchronized movements, expertly passing each other off like batons to the next student in the *be*-ing relay.

Oh my, I think, I'm in trouble here. This isn't exactly home for an introvert.

Miss Trundle catches sight of me and smiles. She is wearing a thick layer of brown lipstick, but no eye-makeup. She clasps her hands happily as if a gift-wrapped package has just arrived.

"A new student!" she clucks. Her diction is perfect, each vowel and consonant distinct and separate.

I mumble an introduction at her prompting. My new classmates shuffle, lift a finger here and there in greeting, mostly eye each other, shaking out their limbs as if for a fight.

"We're preparing to perform Macbeth," my teacher says, hardly able to contain her excitement. "We're a week into it already. I'm afraid you might be a little behind."

"Oh, I've read Macbeth," I say.

Miss Trundle cocks her head and nods: approval. "How lovely! Well, I like to go at things a bit organically. I like to hit the high points first, then come back to pick up the rest. We've made great strides in just a week, covering a lot of the general thrust of the play, but this week we're jumping ahead to Scene four in Act three where Macbeth sees the ghost of Banquo, whom he has had murdered, and Macbeth trembles like a little girl…"

"Ya, Macbeth is a girly-man!" one of the crowd jabs, and a female with high hair and many piercings whacks his arm.

"…and Macbeth's wife, Lady Macbeth, ridicules him just, like, that…"

Miss Trundle unleashes her perfect diction again, her t's standing out like sharp, pointed arrows. She extends a long, freckled finger at the wisecracker, without looking at him, and the pierced girl whacks him again.

"...but this ghost-sighting is a momentous moment: this is Macbeth's epiphany!" Miss Trundle's hand shoots skyward for emphasis.

"Epiffa-what?" This from a sandy-haired boy who a moment ago had been squatting, eastbound then westbound in a low ogre's stride, deep-peeping menacingly.

Everyone laughs, except me.

Miss Trundle smiles, a full, brown-lipped smile. Her freckled eyelids crinkle cheerfully. "Ah, you're nothing but riff-raff," she teases. "Now listen up, class. This young lady has actually read Macbeth." I don't need to be an actor to see from my classmates' body posture that this fact doesn't earn me any brownie points. "Do you, um..."

"Sarah Joanne," I remind.

"Sarah Joanne, can you tell the class what an epiphany is?"

The class goes quiet. Arms crossed. Brows up, eyes on mine.

"She's dirty," someone says from the top tier, behind a wall of bodies.

"An epiphany is a revelation," I say, as quietly as I dare. "A moment of truth, when you finally understand what's important about a person, or a situation. A life-changing moment."

Miss Trundle nods, smiling. The rest of the class nods, too, not so good-naturedly.

"Smart," someone says, as if it's a character flaw.

"Dirty," another repeats.

"Miss Fancy Pants with the big words."

"Big words. Big head." The rumble carries around the room.

I sink inside myself as far as I can go. As soon as Miss Trundle releases me, I take my place on the margins of the crowd, where I wait for class to let out.

***

There are many kinds of ghosts, I figure. It doesn't matter if their existence is ever proven scientifically, or not. They are there: ghosts of dreams, echoes of memories, imprints on your mind. Fossils stamped into the fibres of your body. Sometimes you can even feel other people's ghosts, all around you.

I have read that eighty-five percent of all communication is non-verbal. That means that the words we say to each other make up only a small part of any encounter. It is ghosts that make up the rest. Not real ghosts, maybe, but the unconscious assembly of a puzzle of facial expressions, movements, maybe smells, I don't know. Somehow we pick up things we can not put our fingers on, but inside us we know more than we hear, maybe more than we see.

Some people say we have a third eye that sees more than what our physical eyes see. That makes sense to me. I can be in a place, like this park, be aware of the trees and the sky and the grass around me, and still, in my mind's eye, I can see an entire other world as clearly as if it were right there in front me. Sometimes it is a real world; a memory, for instance. Sometimes it is a memory of a real world twisted into new shapes or events by my imagination. Sometimes, like when I imagine what so-and-so meant when he said that, or how I must look to other people, then it is hard to know what is real and what is me.

The interesting part is that what we see in our imagination is as real to our bodies as what has actually happened. The images we conjure up leave imprints on our bodies, affecting hormonal balances and chemistries in ways I don't quite understand. But you don't need to understand something for it to exist.

Mr. H's lunchtime tests show that I am ideally suited for the vocation of Philosopher. That is all well and good, I think, if you don't need to eat. Has there ever been a firm of philosophers? Could you be Vice President, Ethics division, Philosophers Incorporated? We will continue looking, Mr. H and I, for something more practical.

In the park on this crisp October day, I hide my hands inside my jacket sleeves, they are so chilled against my handlebars. My bike is neither pretty nor new, having been purchased second-hand at a yard sale two years before. My helmet, no doubt, is geeky beyond words, but it beats risking brain-oatmeal if I should fall.

Joseph, in the distance, looks athletic in his shiny streamlined bike helmet with the built-in visor. He is peddling his new bike with unsteady legs. Dad runs behind, one hand on the seat. I can tell from here that they are both smiling. It is a peculiar time to have bought a new bike, this late in the autumn. It's a peculiar time of life to be teaching Joseph to ride: I learnt when I was six, the year after my parents split, but there'd never been any money after that to buy my brother a bike—not when he was six, or seven, or eight. My guess is that dad has just realized that summer has come and gone; he had promised Joseph that "this year I will teach you to ride a bike." Dad would never break a promise: not to Joseph.

Dad and Joseph turn in the distance. Joseph wobbles. Dad holds the seat of the new bike. The corner is wide: it takes them well off the paved path and onto the dying lawn. The front wheel pivots and twists its treads toward me, and Joseph (with dad running behind) picks up speed. Even from here I can see Joseph grin.

"Ha!" he laughs. The sound fires through the wind.

He is headed my way.

Dad says something stern but hopeful; he is frowning, and his fists are clenched as he lets Joseph sail on his own. Dad holds those fists clenched against his bent knees, catching his breath, his big shoulders pointed toward where I am, but not at me: at the back of Joseph's bike, speeding my way.

"Swampy! Swampy Jo! I'm flyin'! Y'can't do THIS on that wreck of a bike YOU got!" Joseph is elated. The closer he gets, the more I can count the slits between his teeth, every one of them spit-washed and gleaming, his lips pulled back like he's never grinned before.

"Yeah, well, you're practically old enough to get your driver's license. I was SIX when I learned to ride a bike." I edge my wreck off the walkway, not trusting the sway in his handlebar axis.

"You NEVER had a bike that went THIS fast!"

Each push of his skinny knees brings him closer. Dad stays back, where he'd launched Joseph into space. My brother is fast approaching the spot where I stand astride my rust-bucket. In two more knee-strokes he'll be past me.

"You remember the first ride I had, Yofus? You were there, in Mom's arms. You remember how Mom ran with me then let me go..."

Joseph's shining new bike zings past me, dragging a flimsy wind in its wake.

"...and everything was going great, and then I looked back at her and hit the neighbour's house? Remember how my baby fingernail flew off in a big arc over my head? How we never found it in the long grass? And all the blood. Remember all the blood, baby brother?"

Joseph's bike wavers, twenty paces past me. The back of his seat moves away from the rear tire, and then abruptly changes direction. The back of his head wavers too, as if he is going to look back at me, or for dad. One more exaggerated waver and then he goes down. Nothing catastrophic: just a bumpy, jumbled tussle between shiny metal and old grass.

Joseph says something rude, and pounds the ground.

Dad strides in front of me, creating a flicker of manmade breeze. He doesn't pause or glance my way. Dad knows you are here, too, I say to myself. From where I stand astride my rusty bike, I feel the hardness of his lack of interest in me.

"Jealousy will get you nowhere, little boy," the voice of a pinched old lady intrudes. A moment passes before I realize that she is speaking to me.

"You mustn't be greedy," the woman continues, "just because that boy's father has given him a new bicycle. Not everyone's got the same income, you know. There's nothing wrong with your bike, even though it's a little worn. I'm sure your father has provided for you as best he can. Be a good boy and appreciate what you have."

She could have smiled but she doesn't.

A meek nod on my part sends her off, satisfied that she has done her societal duty by straightening me out.

It's not the first time I've been mistaken for a boy. It's not the first time someone thinks that dad is not my father. It doesn't matter. As for jealousy...

Something catches my eye, something familiar. A dark-haired couple, tall and elegant, slink down the stone walkway along the water's edge, lost in each other. She is draped around him, her mouth on his neck, her short hair slicked back onto her well-shaped head. His jacket is open, showing his lean torso; he walks with a casual full-bodied stride. Despite the distance, the redness of his mouth stands out: the tip of an iceberg of palpable sensuality. She moves her hand along the landscape of his stomach, tucks her fingertips inside the waist of his jeans.

My middle convulses imperceptibly. It is Paul. Astride my decaying bicycle, square helmet on my head, I watch. It is inevitable that they will see me: I am like a deer caught in their headlights. With each step they take I feel heavier, tied to the earth like some hideous boil. He is coming nearer, nearer, so close now that I can see the lustre of his skin, the shine of his upper lip. In an easy sweep, as though a rumble through the earth alerts him to my presence, he turns those dark, flat eyes on me. No change in stride, his mouth still moving into the mouth of the girl on his hip, her hand still hidden in his waistband, he watches me watching him. A scream builds inside me; I want to bury myself in those lips. I want the earth to swallow me up.

"Crap, it's Swampy Jo!"

I am startled by a voice I know well: it's Madison, her long hair wrung back into an elaborate nest of twists. Her hand jumps out of Paul's jeans to the surer ground of his rib cage.

The smallest whisper of a smile plays at the corner of Paul's lips. He blinks at me, his stare heavy and intimate.

All at once they turn away without another word, up from the walkway to a dense grove of trees, which cluster semi-nude in the autumn sun. Madison is laughing, saying: "Cripes she scared me. Freakin Swampy Jo! She looks like such a knob in that bicycle helmet!"

"She's okay," Paul says abstractedly. "Not quite old enough for me though." He pulls a beeping cell phone from his pocket, looks at the screen, stabs his thumb at a few keys and tucks it away again.

"Pockets!" Madison's shock is barely contained. "She's just a baby, forget her. Dang, she startled me—I'm almost as freaked as I was last night at the party, when you wouldn't wake up. Geez, Pockets, you were bombed! You were too drunk to even barf, man! We thought we'd have to take you to the hospital. If that big hairy friend of yours, Thor or whoever the hell he is, if he hadn't been there to hang you over the balcony and make you puke, I don't know if you'd be here this morning. He had to stick his finger down your throat so far…"

"Stop talking." Paul's voice, far up on the hillside above me now, is thick, low.

The crunch of brittle leaves as their bodies tumble to the ground, somewhere behind the naked nestling trees.

My face is hot with opposing forces of desire and shame. Something aches inside me, something I need to escape, something like hunger. I speed off, pushing hard, hard against the bike pedals, pushing, pushing, very fast now. Over leaves on the pavement, on the stone, leaves blown wildly about by the bicycle tires' lusty advance. Over echoes, shadows, imprints of leaves stamped like fossils on the hard stone beneath. Ghosts of leaves stamped on the earth.

Chapter Two

We are all upstairs at Aunt Cassie's. Ironically, Mom does not like to be in our basement apartment much, though it is now all ordered and pretty, bedecked in tones of rich colour. Joseph is settled, if you can call it that in spite of his constant fidgeting, in front of Aunt Cassie's television in the adjoining living room, watching a rented video full of horror and violence.

"Yofus," Mom reprimands, "don't laugh so hard while you're eating! You'll choke on your food!"

Mom has made Joseph a meal of a peanut butter and jam sandwich, with a side of corn on the cob, which was frozen from last summer's crop. Mom offers the remaining cobs to Aunt Cassie and me. The kernels are blanched and sunken, but dressed in butter and salt, the steaming corn is delicious. This is our supper, served after some delay at nine forty-five at night. Mom eats three cobs, very daintily, with much wiping between mouthfuls.

Out of the corner of my eye, I watch the heroine in Joseph's video cradling a spitting machine gun against her sleek leathered thighs. She is gleefully slaughtering a demon emerging from a swamp, intent on devouring her soul.

Aunt Cassie has been to the library again. Great stacks of books are spread out on the dining table.

"Whatcha got here, Cass?" Mom dabs at her buttered mouth with a carefully folded square of napkin.

"Palm reading!"

Mom's eyebrows go up.

"What?" Aunt Cassie says.

"Nothing. Really."

"C'mon, sis. I know that look."

"No, Cass, really. It's nothing." Mom puts the napkin down, trolls her front teeth with her tongue, in search of stray kernels.

"What? So I like books. What's it to you?"

Mom shrugs. "You're right, Cass. It's nothing to me. You've got a right to read anything you want."

Aunt Cassie stares at the books a minute. Someone dies in Joseph's video. I take another bite of corn, and a trickle of wet butter bleeds into my hands.

"It's not evil, you know."

Mom's hands are up, folded napkin still in place. "Hey, I'm not..."

"Just 'cause we were raised on God doesn't mean that's the only truth there is."

Mom's head is shaking. "No, you're right, I..."

"It's just a new way of looking at things. It could be right.

Who knows? Right?"

"Right."

I chew some more, and the sound is loud in the silence. Someone on television screams.

"It's just that last week it was something else." Mom does some more dabbing before buttering a new piece of corn. "Rune stones, and before that meditation, and Feng Shui. And awhile back it was Tarot cards, and Ouija boards. Oh, and astrology, there was that bit you did with astrology. You're a real do-it-yourself psychic."

"I'm not saying I'm psychic," Aunt Cassie says. "I have no natural talent or anything. It's just something to believe in."

Mom's eyes are big above her cob. "Oh my God, Cass! I actually felt Ma turn over in her grave, there!"

"Oh let's not get melodramatic, sis. It's only palm reading. If it's not true, then what harm can it do? The church won't be any worse for wear for it. And if there IS any truth in it, then maybe we can learn something."

The plastic figure on the kitchen crucifix overhead bleeds red plastic rivulets like a bug pinned for study, the drooping head taking in the heathen imagery below, gaunt features etched with grief. Christ on the cross, hanging from plastic spikes hammered deep into the hollows of his hands. I wonder what Aunt Cassie would have to say about those palms.

The butter on the corn cob in my hands continues to ooze into the lines of my palms, erasing them.

"It's all so fascinating," Aunt Cassie gushes. "The ancient art of palmistry! You can tell everything there is to know about a person just by looking at their palm! The state of their health, their personality. Their future! How old they'll live to be, whether they'll marry... once, or twice, maybe."

A subtle nudge in Mom's direction makes her brighten a bit between mouthfuls of corn.

"You can tell that?" Mom mumbles, cheeks full.

"Yup! It's all here, in these books. Basically you start by examining the whole hand: the shape of it, the length of the fingers compared to the length of the palm. Apparently even the way you hold out your hand says something about you. If your hand is stiff, for instance, it means you're unyielding. You know, stubborn, single-minded, determined, inflexible. All that just from how you extend your hand! So..." Aunt Cassie flips through one book, then another, showing us elaborate illustrations of the components of the hand. "You start with the shape of the hand and its 'aspect.'" Her hidden smile proclaims her pride at this budding understanding of palmistry lingo. "Then you look at the 'phalanges,' which means the sections of each finger."

"Phalanges," Mom winces. "Ugly word."

"Oh for heaven's sake!" Aunt Cassie is frowning.

"Just sounds rude to me. Like a penis or something."

"You mean *phallus*," I say, and Mom's eyes widen, turning her instantly mute.

"So," Aunt Cass continues brightly, "there are three phalanges, or sections, per finger, and two phalanges on the thumb. The comparative length of each section on each different finger gives clues to personality. Each finger represents something different, a different area of interest or character. The baby finger, for instance, is known as..."

A pause as she rummages through pages.

"Yes, here it is. The little finger is also called the Mercury finger. Mercury is the Roman god of commerce and trade, so the baby finger reveals..."

Here she reads right from the text:

"…'the individual's natural instincts.' So, see, if the tip of your little finger is longer than the other two baby finger sections, then that means that you are…"

Another consultation with the book before her.

"…'Charming and unusually perceptive.' Here, this is easier if I have a real hand to work with. Sis?"

Mom extends a ragged cob held wetly between two buttered hands, her mouth too full to speak.

"Well, Swampy Jo: looks like it's you. Your Mom is… unavailable at the moment."

Aunt Cassie takes my hand in both of hers. The golden salve of butter has drenched my palms like holy water. Two shallow pools of yellow now fill the hollow of my hands, upturned and leaking like those of Jesus, crucified. Mom mops at them with paper napkins, her cheeks full of corn. The yellow bleeds into the paper, saturating it in seconds.

"Oh—your hands, Swampy Jo! They're… well, they're so pretty, really. A little ragged, but—well, I just knew you weren't the type to fuss over your hands. The nails are quite short and somewhat crooked. A filing is all you need to clean them up. Here, it will only take a minute."

Aunt Cassie returns with her purse, from which she extracts an emery board. The file slides along my finger tips, rounding the edges of my nails into smooth arches.

"Now see, this gives me time to assess your whole hand. This will give us clues to your basic make-up. Your in-born potential. Your strengths and weaknesses. For starters, I see that your palm is shorter than your fingers. See? If I take a measurement of your middle finger from the base of the palm to the fingertip…"

She holds her fingers apart to show the exact length of

my centre digit, keeps her fingers locked on that distance and moves her hand to compare this finger measurement to that of my palm. The palm is clearly shorter.

"We can see quite easily that your fingers are long, by comparison. Sis, can you read what that says for me?"

Mom wipes her mouth meticulously, in her active slow-motion way, then reads:

"'If the palm is longer, you have short fingers, and vice versa. Roughly equal measurements indicate a well-balanced personality. Individuals with long fingers ...'"

"That would be you, Swampy Jo," Aunt Cassie interjects.

"... 'are introspective, preferring to mull things over before reacting.'" Mom takes another bite of corn.

"So there's clue number one," says Aunt Cassie. "You're a thinker not a doer. Then you look at the width of the hand, to see if the top or bottom of the palm is wider or narrower. The shape and width of the fingers and joints are important too."

Aunt Cassie holds out my hand, appraising it objectively.

"You have more or less a rectangular palm, with long bony fingers with pronounced joints."

A buried volume gets yanked from the pile. A quick thumbing through finds the required page.

"A quick comparison with the drawings in this book, and I would say that you have what is called a Philosophic Hand. You, then, are a thinker (which we already knew from your long fingers), who 'enjoys exploring the subjects of religion, motivation, and the deeper meaning of life. You need a lot of privacy'—ooh, that's too bad, because you mustn't get much here, sharing a room with your mom, and a small house with ... how many of us are there? ... my three plus your three, is six of us. Not exactly oodles of privacy here, is there?"

On cue, Joseph hollers over the movie for fruit punch. Mom quickly obliges.

"If it keeps him quiet," she explains.

"The thumb represents willpower. A stiff thumb means a stubborn person; a supple thumb means a flexible person. You're somewhere in the middle. Not much to tell there."

I must work on that, I think.

"Should I be stubborn or flexible, Aunt Cass? Which is better?"

Aunt Cassie is preoccupied. Her expression as she examines my hands speaks volumes: that non-verbal communication thing, again.

"Mmm? I guess that depends on your circumstances. Bit of each is pro'bly best. But there's more. The narrow angle between your thumb and index finger shows a tendency to introversion…"

A smile of recognition.

"And a vulnerability to stress."

A frown.

"The fact that your baby finger leans in toward your ring finger shows that you have a kind and sympathetic nature."

A nod of approval. More measuring of comparative lengths.

"The fact that your baby finger is set so low on your palm shows a tendency to low self-esteem," and here she keeps her eyes and voice lowered. "This lack of confidence likely stems from childhood experiences."

A shadow over her brow.

Mom returns from her juice errand, threatening Joseph with untold misery should he spill his cup on Aunt Cassie's living room rug. In perfect response, Aunt Cassie's voice brightens, immediately losing its secretive tone.

"This short bottom section to your little finger means that you are trusting and impressionable. Your ring or Apollo finger (Apollo is the god of music and arts) is perfectly balanced, showing that you're very creative. The Saturn finger—that's the middle one, the tallest on your hand—represents money and practical matters. Yours leans toward your ring finger, which indicates a profound need for security, both emotional and material. In other words, you need to feel safe and loved to be at your best."

Again Aunt Cassie lowers her eyes. Her mouth stretches into a grim line, but only for a moment. Mom studiously picks stray kernel husks from the tablecloth, placing them carefully on the edge of her plate, where skeletal cobs lie scattered like bones.

There is something here, the whisper of something that remains unspoken.

"The slant in your Saturn finger also shows that you hate conflict. The long top section means that you're a bit of a detective."

A jump of Aunt Cassie's eyebrows.

"A detective! Your palm says that you are a researcher type, who enjoys finding hidden meanings. Now that sounds like fun! Your index finger, the Jupiter finger, signifies the ego. You see how it leans away from the middle finger? That is the sign of the independent thinker. Good for you! The tip leans in a bit toward the middle though ..." A quick consult brings: "... so you're very cautious."

A moment's hesitation. She does not want to say this next part.

"The length of your index—see how it's shorter than your ring finger? That indicates low self worth. Poor pet."

Her voice is very quiet now. Mom fidgets.

"Now for the good part!" Aunt Cassie says so brightly that I jump. "So far we've looked at the shape of your hand and your fingers, which reveal your basic character. But your palm, now that's where the good stuff is! Your palm shows the events and direction of your life. Your future! Let's start with the skin itself."

She caresses my open palm, helpless as a naked baby. Her hands are toasty warm against my cold ones.

"We all know we have finger prints, right? Those patterns and whorls that make up your finger prints are on your palms too. You can see them, if you look really closely. With the right light…yes, I can see a couple of whorls. Let me see your other hand too. By the way, you're right handed, aren't you, Swampy Jo? That's what I thought. According to what I've read, your writing hand (in this case, your right one) shows what you are actually doing with your life. The opposite hand (with you, that would be your left) shows your potential at birth: your God-given destiny. If you compare both palms," which she does now, "you can sometimes see some startling differences. For instance, you have a whorl print on your palm between your middle and ring fingers: that indicates a wish to help others, coupled with a serious sense of purpose or even a vocation."

"A vocation?" I ask.

"Yes, you know, like a calling. A mission in life. Something you're born to do. Now, that whorl is on both your left and your right palms. So it looks like real life will play out pretty much as it was intended on this point: you're motivated to help others. But there is one other whorl, right here. See? This mound of flesh here—these plumper parts of the hands are called mounts, and they each have a name and a corresponding set of attributes—well, this whorl is on your mount of Luna, curving toward the 'percussion' edge of your palm (that means the outside of your hand). This whorl suggests that you have a 'sixth sense.'"

Aunt Cassie's eyes grow round. Mom sits up and looks at me. Aunt Cassie continues.

"Now isn't that nifty! The fact that the whorl is only on your right hand would mean that this sixth sense is something you develop, rather than an inborn sensitivity."

"My daughter," giggles Mom. "A psychic!"

"A self-*made* psychic," I point out. "That can't possibly be as good as a *born* psychic. It isn't the same thing at all. I can't see how you can develop an intuition like that, a sixth sense about things. It doesn't make sense, does it? Either you have it or you don't, right?"

Aunt Cassie sputters. "My darling niece," she says, "are you implying that learning doesn't count? That, for instance, either you're born with a talent for, say, palm reading, or you're not? Like palm reading's not something you can pick up from, say, a *book*?" Aunt Cassie eyeballs me, her hand on a palm reading book, daring me to discount her.

I stammer something incomplete, the sort of half-baked sentence that Mr. Habbernashy might blurt out.

"Anyway, let your old aunt read the rest of your palm, as imperfect a reading as that may be." Aunt Cassie's eyebrows are twitching, but she's settling down. "I've been doubted by finer folk than you, my friend. Now, let's take a look at the lines in your hands. This line," she tickles a fold in my palm, "is your head line. And this is your heart line. Simple right? Those are clear enough. The Fate line, or line of Destiny, is harder to find. It does not appear in every palm. It would run from the wrist up the palm to the ring finger, although sometimes it stops halfway. Now you, Swampy Jo, have something very curious happening between your heart and head lines, and extending from your Fate line. You've got one, a Fate line, I mean. That's for sure."

Aunt Cassie concentrates on one palm, then the other. She turns the palm into, then away from the light, thoughtfully examining the fine pink lines running along the surface.

"You have something that is very rare, apparently. A very rare mark. Most people don't have it. Do you see it, here? It's the sign of the Mystic…"

Madison bursts into the room, looking effervescent as always, clad in form-fitting denim from head to toe. The rope of her hair twists over one shoulder, shining like black satin against her stone-washed ensemble. The crisp white of her T-shirt echoes the whites of her eyes, her teeth. Quickly, I draw my hands from off the table to hide them in my lap. Caught bare handed.

"Holy! Mom! Are you reading palms? What a blast! Can you do mine? Here, Mom, tell me about myself. Pockets: where are you? Pockets, get your beautiful butt in here!"

Paul straggles into the kitchen, as dark and denimed as Madison. For a nanosecond he looks out of place. But then he smiles, pulls out the manners.

"Evening, Mrs. Bradley," he grins at Mom. To Aunt Cassie, he says: "Mrs. Brighton, how are you?"

"Oh for heaven's sake, Paul, call me Cassie."

"Sure thing, Mrs. Brighton." His grin is at once gentlemanly and bold.

My insides quiver.

Aunt Cassie offers corn (declined) and a seat at the table, which they take, Paul slipping into the chair beside me. The video screeches in the background as the revived demon gains the upper hand.

Beneath the cover of the table, I wipe vigorously at my hands, blotting butter residue from my heart, head and fate lines. All of my peripheral attention is concentrated on Paul, who is eyeing me unabashedly with the cool detachment of a visitor to the zoo. My face reddens, my hands toil on themselves, working in vain. Like a guilty Lady Macbeth endlessly washing invisible blood from her hands.

"My hand, Mom, read my palm!" Madison's eagerness has Aunt Cassie sold within seconds.

"Well, let's see. You have a conic hand: gently rounded, with elegant, tapering fingers with rounded tips. That means," once again the manual is quoted, "'you are artistic, imaginative, and fun loving.' On the negative side," and I think I hear a dismissive tone to Aunt Cassie's voice, "it can also mean that you have many acquaintances, but few really close friends. You can come off as superficial. But," the voice perks up again, "you are generous, and wonderful company."

Madison elbows Paul, as if to say: *See? I told you so.*

Paul is still staring at me. My face reddens; I put my hands to my cheeks and lean forward, feigning interest in Madison's reading.

"These pronounced mounds at the base of your thumb indicate vitality and libido," Aunt Cassie says.

"Libido. That means sex, right?" Madison's enthusiasm fills the entire room, until I am nearly choking on it.

"Yes it does. Specifically, it refers to the sex drive. Yours is quite healthy, even robust," Aunt Cassie says with unexplained pleasure. I can't help thinking that any other parent would discourage such a thing in their child, or would at least make a face, which is what Mom is doing. "And this area beneath your index finger, called the mount of Jupiter, shows high ambition.

You'll have to guard against becoming overbearing or selfish."

The voice of a mother talking. Madison snorts.

Aunt Cassie measures and compares, analyzing phalanges, lines and mounts. I am no longer listening. I am feeling Paul watch me. Feeling the heat that his eyes on me generate. I am enjoying it too much, so much that I must lean away from him as far as possible. I am metal to a magnet, trying to break the field of attraction.

Eventually Madison is satisfied with her mother's interpretation of her fortune, and turns her attention to the next victim.

"Come on Pockets, let's do you."

He hesitates, his hands firmly clasped beneath the table.

"Ladies first," he says. His voice is pure bass.

Mom balks, even though she has been examining her palms, comparing them to everything that Aunt Cassie has outlined.

"We've already done Swampy—I mean Sarah Jo," Mom explains. "I guess that just leaves me, and I'm not really burning to know my future. The present is enough for me to handle at the moment, thanks. You go ahead, Paul. Let's see what life has in store for you."

Reluctantly, Paul allows his hands to be taken hostage within Aunt Cassie's.

"Are you right- or left-handed, Paul?"

"I'm a leftie," he says, colour rising in his face.

"Alright then, let's start with your right—that one's got your destiny in it." Aunt Cassie bobs her eyebrows at Paul, who pushes air through his nose in the guise of laughter.

All four women—Aunt Cassie, Mom, Madison and I—lean in with gusto. Paul remains glued to the back of his chair, his arm extended fully so that the rest of him is removed from the action, his face turned away. Like someone about to undergo an operation without anesthetic. He is not eager to enter our feminine circle.

His hand is very brown. His short fingers, we learn, indicate an impetuous, high energy type who acts quickly. His hand is definitely an Elementary one: not pretty, very square. The hand of a nature lover. His left thumb is held closely to his index, suggesting difficulties in childhood. The middle section of his thumb is shorter than the top: a clear sign of the intuitive type who leaps before looking. A short index finger, shorter than the ring finger, means low self esteem.

A hum of recognition passes between us. I am aware now of his eyes on the floor, the table, the books: anywhere but on me.

A variation in the phalanges of his little finger shows that he is shy. Madison snorts.

"Yeah, right. Not!"

Paul is impassive. If it weren't for his shallow breathing, you might think he wasn't listening.

There is more. Fingerprint loops mean a tendency to emotional extremes, with exaggerated highs and lows. A tented arch print on the index confirms great emotional energy, and a desire to change the world. Madison chimes in.

"How about love lines, Mom. Marriage and all that. What does his palm have to say about that?"

An annoyed squint on Paul's part does nothing to deter Aunt Cassie in her findings.

"There are two places we can look for that. Here," Aunt Cassie deciphers, "rising from the Mount of the Moon toward the Fate line (when there is one) are the Influence lines. They can appear quite suddenly, and are supposed to indicate new relationships. The lines become stronger as attachments deepen."

"So, anything deep yet?" Madison demands.

"No. But there are several faint lines. It seems that some are fading. Maybe one is a little stronger. But I'd be pushing it if I said it was deep."

Madison pouts.

"And these little horizontal lines under the little finger are called Marriage lines, although most books reject them now as inaccurate. Most experts today believe that they indicate all important relationships, not necessarily marriage."

"Times change," Mom says sadly.

"Well," Madison interjects, "are there any Marriage lines in his hand? Forget what the experts say. They're just a bunch of freakazoid palm readers! What does his *hand* say?"

Aunt Cassie peers at the spot for some time.

"Well, to tell you the truth, there really aren't any relationship lines here. I suppose you could count this little mark here, but it's very small and very faint. Hardly what you could call a deep attachment. Well, Paul. I guess you're not the marrying kind."

"Crap," offers Madison.

"You don't really have a clearly defined Fate line, either, Paul. Wait a minute, that's not quite true. If I put your hand to the light I can see it. It's just that your Fate line is very, very faint. Except for here, between the Head and Heart lines. In fact... Swampy Jo, give me your hand. The left, the one that shows your potential. Look at this."

Even Paul leans in this time. Our hands lie side by side in the centre of the table, curved into empty cups. I can feel the delicious heat from his hand, though we are not touching. My hand is as cold as a corpse in a morgue. The multitude of fine lines on our palms spring up under the harsh kitchen light. Specimens under a microscope.

Together we gaze as Aunt Cassie unveils the mystery.

"I was trying to tell you this before Madison and Paul came in, Swampy Jo. What you have between your Heart and Head lines is a very rare marking. You see these two lines that criss-cross, forming a letter x? That mark is called the Mystic Cross, or sometimes the Psychic Cross. It indicates the influence of the unexplained on your life. When it's linked to the Heart line, it means you may have a superstitious nature. If it's linked to the Head line, you may be uncommonly aware of the supernatural forces around you. According to these books, not only is the mark itself rare, but rarer still will it touch both the Heart and Head lines. And," Aunt Cassie continues breathlessly, "most unusual is the fact that your Fate line connects directly to this Mystic Cross. They are all infinitely inter-connected: the Head, Heart and Fate lines. Your mind, your heart, your destiny. You are one in a million. Something very special, very mysterious, is in store for you Swampy Jo."

My hand, holding this miracle of the Mystic Cross marking, lies helplessly on the table, growing colder. Aunt Cassie is not yet done.

"There's more. Now look at Paul's hand. See the Heart line here. And the Head line. See how the cross, that same mark of the Mystic Cross, joins the two? As if the x formed a support beam that keeps both the Heart and Head lines anchored. Almost as if your sanity, Paul, your emotions, your very life, even, all hinge on this Mystic Cross. And then," Aunt Cassie is giddy with discovery, "with Paul's hand in the direct light here, can you see? Can you see how this Mystic Cross lines up perfectly with his Fate line? Your destiny is clearly shaped by this Mystic Cross, this link with the other-worldly. Compare the two hands, Swampy Jo's and Paul's. The same markings are found on both! What are the chances of finding this particular assembly of markings on one hand, let alone two? All I can say from this is that you two must be linked somehow. Your destinies are somehow psychically linked."

She looks from Paul to me, trying to puzzle it out. "There must be something about the two of you that—I don't know—something that completes the other. Some kind of psychic circuit, maybe? I don't know. One thing's certain: the presence of the supernatural has something to do with your Fates, maybe even with your actual minds and hearts. The very things that keep you alive, that make you who you are. I've never seen anything like it!"

Not that Aunt Cassie's experience is very vast.

Paul eyes the criss-cross of lines in the middle of his hand, in the middle of mine, which sweats butter in response. Our hands lie inches apart, like exhausted lovers. "Like the cross-hairs in the sights of a gun," he says.

The thought scares me, thrusts me back in my chair briefly.

"Kinda," I admit. "More like a star, I think."

"A Mystic Cross," Aunt Cassie says reverently.

"What d'ya know," he says. His brown eyes are dark as pitch under the umbrellas of his heavy lids.

"Pockets, are you going to fall in love with Swampy Jo?" Madison pouts. Her lovely face contorts in disbelief. Paul's easy laugh denies it. Still, I catch an invisible flash of anger, or fear maybe, on his face, or maybe just the threat of it. I am suddenly aware of a ghost of rage behind those dark hooded eyes. The snap of a whip, and it's gone.

"Well, on that note," he says amiably, putting his hands in his pockets, "why don't we try to catch a late show? What do you say, Madison."

She quickly agrees. They are off, as ebullient as when they arrived, as though the earth hadn't just opened up.

I hold my Mystic Cross palm in my ordinary hand, as though it were something precious and fragile and full of promise. As though it were something glorious.

Mom stirs. She has been staring at her own palms for a long time now, comparing what she sees with Aunt Cassie's comments.

"All this talk of the psychic, the supernatural. Maybe it's just another way of looking at the whole God thing. I'm sure a few priests I know would go into convulsions over the thought, but maybe the occult is just the whispering of angels, prodding you this way or that, or protecting you."

I imagine the crucifix over Aunt Cassie's kitchen door hurling itself down to burn a hole in the library of palmistry books on the table.

"Whatever you call it, I've had a visitation, or something. I think of it as my guardian angel. It was the day your dad left. Do you remember, Swampy Jo? You were so little—five years old I think, wasn't it? So long ago. Yofus was in bed: he was still just a baby. The day had been so long. So hard. I could hardly move. I made dinner, and the kitchen was a mess. I couldn't think straight. There were dishes everywhere, dirty pots, leftovers. I couldn't face it. I just sat there, trying to get up the courage to move. And then you came in, Swampy Jo, drenched in mud from your toes to your eyebrows. I've never seen anyone so dirty. At first I wasn't even sure it was you. All I could see was your blue eyes peering out from this layer of caked muck. I took you upstairs to the bath, got the water running, somehow peeled off your clothes, which were so stiff they could have stood up on their own. I had to hose you down just to get to where I could at least see your skin. Then I had to empty the bath and start all over again, the bath water was so murky. It took forever to get you clean.

"I remember kneeling by the tub, scrubbing at your hair, trying to find you under all that dirt. I prayed: please God, show me a sign. Help me just to get through this night; if I can just get through this one night, I'll be okay. I've never prayed so hard.

"Well, He did answer me. When you were finally clean—it took so long, you had to soak in the water forever just to loosen up the crud—I got up from beside the tub to dry you off and get you to bed. Once you were settled in, I went into the kitchen. I was exhausted. I was just going to turn off the kitchen light; I figured I would face the dirty dishes in the morning. I had nothing left in me. But when I got there, the kitchen was spotless: all the dishes were clean, put away in the cupboards. The table had been wiped, the floor had been swept. The whole room was perfect. I knew it was an angel that came to help me, an angel I prayed for with all my might just to get me through to the next day. There was no other explanation. The door was locked as it always was. I certainly hadn't done the dishes before I went up to run the bath. It had to be my guardian angel. I just kept saying: thank you God, thank you God.

"You know, whenever I get discouraged, when I think I just can't take one more step, I remember that clean kitchen. If I ever need help, really need it, then it will come. I'm sure of it. I know in my heart that I am taken care of."

I don't know why I say it: it is so cruel. All at once I get so furious, so red-hot angry at my mother's silliness.

"I remember that day." My heart quickens even as the words hit my tongue. "I remember it perfectly. You fell asleep, leaning on the edge of the bathtub. I watched you for awhile, while I played in the tub. But after a bit the water got cold, so I got out. I wrapped myself in a towel. I heard someone, a woman's voice humming in the kitchen, so I went to see. It was our neighbor, Mrs. Fenton. She said that she'd knocked at the door earlier, then come in when no one answered. The door was unlocked, she knew, because she had seen me playing on our beach just minutes before.

"She said she got the feeling something was wrong because dad wasn't home, and I was up so late, unsupervised by the water. She wanted to see if she could help. She said she had called out your name. She could hear us talking upstairs, but Mom, you didn't hear her over the sounds of the bath water running. So she just set to cleaning up the kitchen, which she could see needed doing, humming so that you wouldn't be startled when you came back down. She was just emptying the dust pan when I found her. She hugged me and told me to wake you up so that you could get to bed. She didn't want to stay because she knew you'd feel you had to explain. So she just left, locking the door behind her. It wasn't your guardian angel that cleaned the kitchen, Mom. It was Mrs. Fenton."

A person can deflate all at once, I know now, or simply spring such a slow leak that the loss of air is hardly noticed. Mom just looks at me a very long time. Aunt Cassie babbles:

"Well, a helpful neighbour is as good as a guardian angel any old time. More reliable in fact. In a way, she *was* an angel that night."

But Mom is having none of it. Her whole face droops. She manages a crooked smile.

"Well," she says softly, "I had better get Yofus off to bed. I can't believe he could have fallen asleep in front of a massacre movie. Kids. Thanks for the night's entertainment, Cass."

Mom turns to me, looking me straight in the eye. With a sheepish smile brimming with kindness, she says "Good night, Swampy Jo," and she carries Joseph's sleeping form down the stairs to his bed.

The room hums, full to bursting with silence. When I cannot stand it a moment longer, Aunt Cassie hisses, barely audibly, so that my mind has to fill in her words after they are spoken.

"How could you, Swampy Jo?" she asks. "How could you?"

Chapter Three

I somehow get to bed that night; I guess it's around midnight or so. First, Aunt Cassie and I clean up the tea cups, the corn plates, Joseph's snack emporium by the stack of videos near the TV. We don't say much, we just scrub, like its spring cleaning or something: the table, the counters, the sinks. The toaster oven, which no one even used that day. When the entire kitchen is disinfected and the living room is spotless, we say goodnight without looking at each other, going our separate ways.

My hands are bald and dry. I keep them balled up by my sides, in case the miracle lines within them might escape, shaken loose by each step on the stairs.

It is very quiet in our apartment downstairs. The only sounds are of water sloshing in the pipes hidden in the ceiling overhead; my guess is that Aunt Cassie is now attacking the bathroom. (There is something about the women in my family and bathrooms. Surely it's not normal for people to spend this much time scouring bathrooms that are already clean.) I make a pit stop in our bathroom, too, to give the sink and toilet bowl a swipe in an act of solidarity. Then I wash my hands—I scrub and scrub—and still the Mystic Cross remains. I cannot make it go away. I cannot make it mean anything.

Joseph is asleep, I can tell by his breathing as I pass the door to his room. As quietly as possible, I slink into the room I share with Mom. It will make less noise if I just sleep in the day's clothes, so I slip under my covers in one easy sweep. Mom is not asleep, I can tell, although she doesn't move or make a sound. Her breathing is shallow, controlled, as if she is trying not to breathe at all. Like someone fighting pain.

It is very hard to sleep with shame crowding in on you. By morning I feel worse than at bedtime.

Mom still does not move, though she is awake, I see. Her eyes are locked on the high window in the corner of our room, away from me, away from all of us. She never does get out of bed that day, although each time I check on her she is clearly conscious.

"I suppose she's just catching up on all the sleep she's lost lately," affirms Aunt Cassie with confidence.

"It's true that Mom is sleep deprived," I admit, this rationalization easing my guilt a little. "By my tally, she gets by on three or four hours a night, with the occasional seven-hour sleep thrown in for good measure."

"Mm-hmm," Aunt Cassie agrees. "She's done that most every night for nine years now. It wouldn't be surprising if she just conked out and slept for a solid week."

We share an empty chuckle.

"But she's not sleeping," I confess. "She's ... just lying there."

Aunt Cassie hovers all day, going up and down the basement stairs, offering Mom food, company. Mom cannot manage even to shake her head.

The following day echoes the first, that first day that Mom stopped moving. Her eyes remain locked on the thin strip of gray sky through our high corner bedroom window. Still the shallow breathing of a wounded animal.

"Mom," I say, "at least get up to go to the bathroom."

But as I settle on the edge of the bed and reach out my hand to touch her hip under the covers, I realize she has already gone: the bedspread is soaked with urine.

I change the bed sheets alone, change my mom, who is barely able to roll over. Someone has switched off her power source. That someone is me.

"Maybe she is sick," I tell Aunt Cassie. "She doesn't even cry." The biggest part of me has sunk within the earth and I am heavy as solid lead.

At ten after nine that night—ten minutes after Joseph's bedtime—my baby brother calls 911 in a sudden panic.

"Mom would say goodnight to me," he explains, "if there wasn't something really wrong. It's been two days now, Swampy Jo. Mom can't even see me."

The ambulance attendants, without ceremony, carry my mother up the stairs and out the door. She lies on the stretcher just as she had in her bed. Deflated.

"It's probably for the best," Aunt Cassie says, looking uncertain.

Joseph sleeps in Mom's bed that night. I wake up frequently to look at him, to make sure he's alright; often, he's awake too, staring back at me. Neither of us wonders out loud what will happen next.

***

"Cassandra, for God's sake, mind your own business! This has nothing to do with you. This is my family we're talking about."

"It's my family too. She's my sister. I..."

"They are my children. What the hell do you people think? That I would just forget that fact? You have no goddamn right to keep them, and you know it."

I can hear the fury in dad's voice blaring through the telephone line from where I sit in Aunt Cassie's living room, leafing through one of Madison's fashion magazines. Artfully arranged girls with toothy smiles and spindly legs prance and pose on the pages. *Will he be yours?* the caption says, *Do you have what it takes to make him love you?*

"But you don't understand," Aunt Cassie pleads. "They have just settled in here. They've missed one day of school already, and Swampy Jo..."

"Her name is Sarah Joanne, for Christ's sake!"

My father's anger makes the receiver shake in Aunt Cassie's hand. Without looking, without really even listening, I can sense that there is something she is not saying, something she is too afraid to say to dad.

The argument continues: round two, then three. Aunt Cassie outlines all the logical reasons we should stay. In a last desperate effort she tries:

"My sister wouldn't like it. She told me..."

Dad is formidable, immovable. His rage booms through the telephone line. His determination crests with:

"I don't give a flying f--- what your sister told you. Cassandra, I am coming to get my children NOW!"

In spite of the knot in my middle, in spite of the fear in my throat, a smile is cresting and I have to frown deeply to dismiss it. At least he wants me, my heart whispers.

Aunt Cassie is beside herself, almost in a panic.

"Help me pack your things, Swampy Jo. Your father's on his way. We only have a few minutes." Her trembling betrays tears just beneath the surface.

Downstairs she is frantic in her movements: apocalypse has come.

"Swampy Jo," Aunt Cassie begins. Her voice is a tight whisper, though there is no one around us who could possibly overhear. "Swampy Jo, there's something important you need to know. About your dad. About your dad and you. That day your dad left."

Aunt Cassie's hands work furiously, cramming Joseph's clothes into a canvas bag now. I didn't know that Aunt Cassie, who is usually so meticulous, was capable of cramming.

"It was your Mom who... she found out—it was something that you said. You were just a child, but still—you wouldn't have said it if..."

Aunt Cassie is frazzled, coming apart at the seams. Her eyes are wild with... what? Grief? Rage? Terror?

"Your mother asked your dad to leave. Told him to go, in fact. Because of you. She was afraid..."

We have run out of time. Dad's heavy boots hit the floor overhead. He has not bothered to knock, but instead has strode right into Aunt Cassie's kitchen.

"Cassandra," he booms overhead. "I'm here for my kids."

Aunt Cassie's eyes, large and shining, lock onto mine for one brief, horrible moment. What is it in those eyes? What is she trying to tell me?

"I'm just getting their things," she bellows back. "Yofus is in the backyard, playing. I haven't told him yet. I…We'll be up in a minute."

Turning to me, her voice is gentle, laced with the steely undertone used to inspire a fearful child on the first day of school. That no-turning-back, you-have-to-do-this voice that means there's no way out.

"Swampy Jo, get your things. You mustn't keep your father waiting. You'll be staying with him for…awhile. Until your mother gets better. I don't know how long that will be. Be a good girl." Again that pleading, hard stare. "You will be fine. Just do as you're told, stay out of the way."

What could her emphasis on those last words mean? *Stay out of the way.*

Dad is holding Joseph, who is plumped up with pride and happiness: a prince in the king's arms.

"We're going to live with my Daddy," he announces.

That is how it happens, on an ugly Monday afternoon in bitter November.

It gets worse. On the way to dad's house we stop at the hospital, to see Mom.

When we arrive at the reception desk—my father, brother and I—dad asks to see his wife. *Does he still think of her that way,* I ask myself, *even though they are divorced?*

"Bradley, Psychiatric ward," the receptionist reads from the registry.

The barren halls are cold, smelling of disinfectant. Everywhere I look, I see nothing but sick people. I suppose that is as it should be, in a hospital. But it makes me uncomfortable. Joseph feels it too: he presses his shoulder into my midriff, like a gangster protecting his back.

On the third floor, dad gets further directions from a nurse, who sends us up a hall to a ward room.

"Not a ward anymore," dad commands the nurse. "A single room from now on." And to himself, he mutters: "I'll be damned if I'm going to visit my wife with a roomful of loonies watching."

Instinctively we do our best to keep quiet as we navigate the labyrinth of halls to Mom's room. Our heels click on the hard polished floor, *click click click*, like a clock, or a bomb, ticking. All too soon we reach the doorway. Fear jumps up like vomit in my throat. At first I cannot find Mom in the jumble of rumpled beds and rumpled faces. The eyes that turn toward us are round and vacant, rimmed with sadness, fear, confusion. Every single one of the patients is having her worst hair day. *No curling irons, mirrors or razors are allowed,* a sign by the only bathroom declares, *for reasons of personal and public safety*. That explains it.

A doctor walking by the door hesitates, asks dad who we are trying to find. A handshake and quick introductions follow. I hear words that are overwhelming in their complexity: catatonic state, schizophrenic episode, clinical depression. I am lost in the words and do not even know how to listen, how to decipher this new world my mother is drowning in.

The only pair of eyes that do not fasten on us as we approach are Mom's. She remains cocked in the identical position she assumed on the First Day: back flat to the mattress, arms limp at each side, head turned to the window, gazing at the colourless November sky. Others lying in their beds, I note, are curled into the fetal position; Mom, it seems, does not have the energy even to curl protectively into herself. Helpless. Completely vulnerable. As if the worst, the last blow, has already come.

I think: *dad will go to her*. I think: *that's why we've come*. But he stays planted where he is, even after the doctor has gone, his heavy feet rooted to the centre of the room. Like an evil superhero, he shoots hate vibes throughout the room, causing the bedridden to curl further into their sheets.

Joseph, too, who a moment ago was ready to spring to Mom's side, is frozen to the spot.

I am not a brave person. But sometimes even a worm will come out from his dirty little hole during a rainstorm, if all his hiding places are clogged with water and he will drown if he stays put. In an act of ridiculous courage, I step outside dad's hate force field. My heels click on the hard linoleum. My hand slips inside Mom's: I am surprised at its warmth. Perhaps her thumb moves once along my fingers, or perhaps she just intends it to. It's hard to be sure. Her face seems wearier for the effort.

In the millisecond it takes to touch her hand, my father is gone. He and Joseph are nowhere in the room. Disproportionate fear pumps through me, and my heels slap the floor hard as I tear from the room, down the empty hall.

I find dad hunched over the reception counter, harassing the nurse who had directed us earlier. His voice is muted, strangely, by the fluorescent lights, the thick stench of cleanliness, the hard shiny bare surfaces. I cannot decipher his words but the meaning is clear: she should not be here, the woman who was once his wife. This is not acceptable. But I suspect it is not the staff's decision my father objects to, it is my mother's weakness. The inconvenience of it. The embarrassment. His tirade finished, he turns on me. The laser beam of his anger zeroes in on the place between my eyes. A quiver passes between his eyebrows, like a crack in an iceberg. There is more here: anger, yes, but also… worry. I am mute with shock.

The ride to dad's house is deathly quiet. Dad broods darkly behind his sunglasses. Joseph quivers like a tuning fork that has found the right pitch; the only reason he does not sing with anticipation at Life With Dad is that built-in kid sensor that says don't-bother-your-father-now. Joseph's back is straight as a rail, his eyes shining with yearning for dad's attention. Even his concern for Mom cannot dampen this enthusiasm at having his dad for such a long stretch of time. My heart goes out to my kid brother. I know that kind of bare need: it is a vulnerable thing, standing naked and wanting before someone like that. Someone who might not come through, who might turn his back on you. Of course, it might be different this time. For Joseph.

I smoulder silently, alone in the back seat.

Supper is the most painful thing about the day. The food is beautiful: glistening glazed chicken, the fluffiest mashed potatoes with a sprinkling of parsley on top. The broccoli on my plate (an expensive platter with gold edging and turquoise and purple birds along the rim) is dressed in lemon and herbs, and fills my mouth with bursts of pure green. The salad is a minefield of almonds, mandarins and raisins. There is gravy, and biscuits, and even dessert: a plump lemon cheesecake with berries bursting with syrup on top.

Each swallow is a torture. It does not seem right to be feasting, when Mom is wasting away on a lonely hospital cot. I force myself not to finish, self-denial filling my belly like restitution.

I have never been this close to one of my dad's accessories before. This one—Carla, I'm reminded—is blond. Unnaturally so. A quick peek at the cleavage escaping her blouse tells me that more than her hair has been enhanced. She looks barely older than Madison, though she tells me she is twenty-eight.

"I work for the local television station," she beams. "As the anchorwoman. I do the news."

She flutters her eyelids. I didn't think anyone actually did that in real life.

Joseph is impressed. Dad is silent, devouring his meal without looking at any of us. It is interesting how you can be present in a group of people, all the while giving off the sense that you are not there at all.

I thank Marla—Carla—for the dinner. Looking at my plate she declares:

"But you've hardly touched a thing! I thought teenagers ate like horses."

The fact that my mother is probably dying in a hospital bed seems too trivial to mention; it would take too much explaining. Carla's heavy-lashed eyes settle on me.

"Oh!" she smiles, as though she's just figured it all out. Her handsome manicured hands flutter in the air. "I know just what you mean. I'm always watching my weight too."

She goes on a bit, but I have stopped listening. My mind is screaming.

Joseph excuses himself, too. He has cleaned his plate, except for the salad, which he says politely "... has too much junk in it."

Carla is our hostess now, showing us our rooms, getting extra blankets. She even has brand new toothbrushes for us, laid out in the bathroom that Joseph and I will share. Every room we enter is lovely, tidy and decorated to the hilt. There is the occasional dust ball, I notice, in the corners, and water marks on the mirror. A fine veil of dust coats the carefully displayed guest towels. There is a scale, too, Carla points out, in case I might want to weigh myself.

Carla bids us goodnight and disappears behind the master bedroom door. I hear dad's voice in there, deep and warm for her. The idea that she would stay the night has not occurred to me. It is too awful.

I hide in the bathroom, trying to rub my frantic feelings away with a dry facecloth, trying to bury my filth inside my own skin. I do not dare look at the lines in my hands.

Dad is in Joseph's room; I can hear the two of them through the adjoining door. Joseph is laughing his hearty, happy laugh: the one reserved for tickling. Their voices move about the room: it must be airplane time. (I wish Joseph would *grow* already, so that this ritual could finally be abandoned.) Joseph hits the bed, his negligible weight barely causing the springs to bounce. Their voices are low now. My guess is that they're together on the bed, Joseph tucked in tight, dad's head on the pillow beside his. I remember how dad would always do that.

I head back on tiptoe to my room. Of course it is silly, but for a moment I think dad will come in to say goodnight, to rest his head beside mine on our pillow and whisper about the day, to plan out a dream for the night to come, and imagine something hopeful for tomorrow. To comfort me, maybe, about Mom; to say it's not my fault, it will be okay. I think it without thinking, if you know what I mean.

The click of Joseph's door means dad's headed my way. I can hear his lumbering movements in the dark hallway. My light is out too, so I can barely see his face when he stops at my door: just shades and shapes of gray on gray.

I should have known.

"Goodnight, Sarah Joanne," he says with all the formality of a telephone salesman repeating a name in order to remember it.

That is all there is.

Outside my window, the wind mutters secrets. Angry painful secrets that I cannot understand.

***

"So—Sarah Jo, that's it—how are... things?"

Mr. Habbernashy is smiling his ugliest, friendliest troll smile. We are seated, he and I, in his office once again, on my lunch hour. Mr. Habbernashy's lunch tray perches atop a filing cabinet by the door; it is headed for the cafeteria on his next trip out, as it is laden with an empty bowl, plate and glass that just recently held soup, sandwich and milk. The clock above it reads twelve-oh-five; Mr. H, it seems, cannot manage to postpone his lunch until the lunch hour. He grins a well-fed, satisfied grin.

"Things are fine Mr. H," I lie.

He frowns, hooded eyebrows forcing his beady eyes to become beadier still.

"Are you sure, Sarah Jo?"

"Yes. Of course. Why?" A speck of nervousness grows in me. "Are my marks dropping?"

I have always held the top marks in every subject, in every grade I've ever been in. Always. The thought of losing that edge makes me queasy. It is the one thing that has always been sure.

Seeing my concern, Mr. H is all horrible smiles again.

"Oh no, no, Sarah Jo. That's not—oh, I doubt that that's ever likely to happen. My goodness."

He rubs his ample chin with a fat finger. This is his thinking pose, or as he would say, his muddling-it-out pose. There is something distinctly Winnie-the-Pooh-ish about him.

This 'What is wrong with Sarah Jo?' game does not interest me. The potential list is so long that I dare not begin. I search my mind for topics of conversation that might steer him in a new direction. Unfortunately, I am not quick enough on my toes, and Mr. Habbernashy charges again.

"So how are things going... at home, for instance, Sarah Jo?"

"Fine, thanks."

"You've settled into your new place alright? Your mother, where is she working?... Oh no, that's not right. She's in school, isn't she? Taking university classes? That's a fine ambition, that is, higher learning. Hmm?"

"Yes. Well, no," I hesitate. "I mean, she's sick at the moment. In hospital."

"Ohhh," Mister H says, drawing out the word. "That's too bad, Sarah Jo. I didn't know that. Is it serious?"

I don't know how to answer that. I stretch out my mouth and squeeze myself together, forcing my shoulders up. It's the best I can do.

"Mmm. Has she got a good support system, your mother?"

I don't know again. Another squished shrug.

"She has my Aunt Cassie. And Joseph and me."

Mr. H nods. "Has she got a strong faith? Something she believes in? Your mother."

I think of palm reading and bleeding plastic crucifixes and toilet cleaning and false angels.

"Maybe not anymore," I say.

Mr. H leans back in his chair, which groans and squeaks. He looks at his mismatched ceiling tiles, as if wisdom lives there.

"That's tough," he says. "Makes it hard going if you don't have something to believe in."

"Do you think it can make you sick? Not believing?" I ask.

Mr. H rocks his head, his ugly face stretched across its length, eyebrows up, corners of his mouth down. "Could be, could be," he says. "If you know what an individual believes, then you begin to know an awful lot about who that person is. About why that person does the things he or she does."

It is my turn to frown. "How do you know what to believe? How do you know what's real?"

Mr. H nods vigorously, and his chair squeaks a responding soundtrack. "That's the question, now isn't it, that—very good ... quite." He looks at his rows of books. At a chart on the walls of Maslow's Hierarchy of Needs. At the plastic brain on the corner of his desk. At a framed quotation, which he reads aloud:

"'I believe in intuition and inspiration. Imagination is more important than knowledge.' Albert Einstein."

"Hmm," I say, wishing this had helped. "Sounds random."

More nodding. "Maybe. But what if intuition is less random than everything else?" He looks at me with round eyes, which I take as a sign that I'm supposed to answer.

"You mean gut feelings are more of a sure thing than facts?"

Mr. H grins as if I've just revealed the meaning of life. His jowly face is fat and shining: he's a veritable Buddha. "You, Sarah Jo, have a sensitivity to the subtle. I'm certain of it. I've read your file. I've seen the results of these personality and intelligence tests we've been taking, you and I. You are not a follower. You are a leader."

Me? A leader?

As if on cue, a flock of flittering females sweeps by the door, highlighted hair extensions flying, tiny fists held high, whitened teeth sparkling behind lightening-quick lips. A few black-rimmed white eyeballs flash our way.

"Ohmygawd, ohmygawd," the flock says in multiple voices, "there's that scuzzy girl, like, right there! The crazy bad hair girl! Is she in trouble again? What is her story? Ohmygawd!" Their mincing steps shuffle them away.

"Me. A leader. Give your head a shake, Mr. H," I say, surprised at my own rudeness.

Mr. H launches a snorting, sloppy laugh.

"Maybe not your traditional kind of leader, Sarah Jo: the kind who needs to be at the centre of things. But you can also lead from the sidelines. You can see what's really going on with people, sometimes better, from the sidelines. That's where intuition can kick in. Have you thought of making friends with those girls? They could really benefit from your unique perspective."

I smile, scrunching my nose. "Oh," I say. "I don't know, Mr. H."

"They seem curious about you." He says this gently, like it's a selling point.

"I'm not sure our perspectives ... meld," I say haltingly. "My intuition says: pass on this one."

Mr. H sits back in his chair, makes a steeple of his thumbs and index fingers. "Ah," he says, "shame. For them." His smile is sincere.

Who is this odd man? Gandhi, before the loin cloth?

"So, I've got a treat for you today, Sarah Jo," Mr. H says. "Another test!"

"Woohoo," I deadpan.

"This one's called True Colors. It's a fun test, usually done in groups ..."

Immediately, fate parades a brood of black-garbed boys by the office door, their strides long and swanky. "Yo," one of them says, thrusting a thumb in my direction, "the chick with the big words. What's that about, y'think?"

"Madison's something-er-other," someone informs, popping up first to get a bead on me.

"Oww, Mad-dee-sun!" A chant begins, causing no end of jutting and strutting in the hallway traffic.

Mr. H gets up and closes the door, leaving only a thin crack for an opening.

"I'm more of the loner type, Mr. H," I say, just in case he's brain dead.

"Yes, yes," he says, "you haven't found your niche, yet. Perfectly understandable. These things take time. You're new to the school. Besides, my feeling is you haven't found a real peer group. Hardest to do for the brightest ones, it seems. One of life's idiosyncrasies, perhaps... well, in any case. Socially, you tend to move outside the popular circles: different values, perhaps?"

When I don't answer, Mr. H continues: "Some people tend to strive for the most obvious, least satisfying things, don't they? Young people, especially." He waffles. "Maybe not. Adults are pretty fixated on gathering, gathering, too." He makes scooping motions with his beefy hands. "Gathering things like money. Or control. Possessions. Physical beauty. Good things, sure, nothing wrong with those things, but... there are other things, too, maybe old-fashioned things. Like integrity. Kindness. Peace. More elusive things, harder to grab because you can't see them. But in my opinion, more worth having. I suspect these might be the things you want too, Sarah Jo... Mmm?"

I can't find an answer anywhere in me.

"But there are things in life you can't predict. Little messy things that life throws at you. Illness. The loss of a loved one. Things that, no matter how strong you are, you cannot control. Then what? Are you a loser, if your wife gets sick and you need to curb your plans to care for her?"

The wavy line of Mr. H's brow makes me wonder if, in fact, that is why this passionate scholar is conducting personality tests on dull students out of a tiny high school office in this hard, rock-infested city.

"No, no, I can accept that I don't know it all, that I do not have it all in hand. Don't know a fraction of what life's all about, really." This ignorance of his seems to give him immense pleasure. "There is a certain relief in recognizing your place in the scheme of things: significant, just as worthy as the next guy, but not pivotal. The whole picture is still more or less a mystery to me! It boggles my mind!"

I can picture Mr. Habbernashy as a mind, boggled.

"Well, in any case," he concludes, "everyone sees life their own way, now don't they? I suppose in the end, it doesn't matter much which road you take, if they all lead to the same end. But that's the tricky part, isn't it? Do they? All lead to the same end, I mean. If they don't—well!—then the only thing that matters is what you believe. It's a kind of fundamental programming that affects every single thing that goes thereafter. Without it... well!"

I think of Mom, crippled in a hospital bed because I erased the possibility of a guardian angel who does dishes by night, affecting every single thing that goes thereafter.

"I know what you mean," I whisper. "But what happens if you change your mind? What if something you believed in turns out not to be true?"

Mr. H's voice rumbles with sympathy: "Well, then, that would be a blow, now wouldn't it? You'd be at some loss, until you found something to replace that misguided belief. Preferably, something a little more accurate. Many a successful business man has suffered depression once he has reached his goal, the 'worthy' thing he's struggled his whole life to attain, only to find that what he dreamed would be so wonderful didn't actually change anything at all. Then he doesn't know where to turn, where to put his energies. He has to try all over again to find that thread of truth that runs through all of us. Tricky stuff. Bit of a puzzle, this whole Meaning of Life thing, now isn't it?"

Now my mind is boggled, too.

"Let's get started on this test, shall we?" Mr. H opens a desk drawer and rummages through stacks of paper, like a dog on the trail of a T-bone. "The True Colors test builds a colour profile, ranking your responses in order of preference. Personality characteristics are linked to each of four colours: blue, green, gold, or orange, to provide a picture of you, the individual, as a whole. It's an assessment based on the Myers-Briggs, originally developed by an educator working with troubled high school students"—he doesn't even pause here, oblivious that he's dropped an atom bomb—"but now True Colors is used for everything from career planning to team building..."

"Mr. H," I interrupt, "Mr. H, I'm not sure I'm up to this one today. Can we get to it tomorrow? Or next week, maybe?" My stomach is a knot, digesting visions of Mom sinking into a hospital mattress, completely shut down.

Mr. H stops his rummaging, jump-started back to his role as counsellor instead of fearless psychological explorer.

"So your mother is hospitalized, is she, Sarah Jo? In whose care are you while your mother is in hospital? And you have a younger brother too, don't you?"

"Yes," I say. My mouth is very dry. "My brother is staying with my father, until my mother is well again. I am living with my aunt and her family."

This is the painful truth. After one night at dad's, he informs me as he drops me off at school that I will be returning to Aunt

Cassie's on the afternoon school bus, as I had done before Mom took ill. Joseph will be staying with him, dad says.

That is all there is to know.

"I see," says Mr. Habbernashy soberly. The afternoon bell sounds, announcing a return to classes. Once he has assured me of his availability, should I need anything, anything at all, I am reluctantly dismissed.

Chapter Four

Time passes, not as horribly as you might expect. Aunt Cassie allows me the privacy I crave like air. I prepare my own meals: mostly cold cereal and microwave mac-and-cheese. But the stamina it takes to chew, the calm it takes to swallow without strain, tires me, and soon even the rumble in my belly is not motivation enough for the effort. I sleep when I feel like it, fighting slumber like a child afraid of darkness, until it overtakes me at my weakest.

To pass the time, the television remains on most of the time. In the afternoons, fat girls jiggle down the runways of every talk show, thrusting their ample cleavage at the booing crowds. The ugliest parts of their lives are spelled out in flashing headlines: 'Girls Who've Slept Their Way to an 'A,' 'Sluts of the Slums,' and other such trash. In the evenings, perky interchangeable blondes, brunettes and redheads bounce through picturesque sitcom sets, without the slightest jiggle.

I stare at my hands for long periods, seeing the image of Paul's etched palms super-imposed over mine. Endless, breathless pockets of time, during which I bathe in a mysterious, lingering pain that constricts my ribcage with tears and laughter and longing and a new, unexplored bliss.

Before long though, Aunt Cassie insists I need more people contact.

"It's okay for you to sleep down there alone," she says, "and even to do schoolwork and watch TV alone. I know how important your privacy is to you. But you do need to spend some time with us. Too much time alone can make you loopy. Come and eat with us upstairs tonight. "

I concede. The gnawing in my middle tightens in anticipation of a real meal.

"Weddings are just gorgeous," Madison gushes over her dinner plate, clearly indulging her ridiculous schoolgirl fantasies. "I can't wait to get married. I'll have the most beautiful gown—you'll make it for me, won't you Mom?" she asks Aunt Cassie, who beams. "Something cinched in at the waist, because that's my best feature, my tiny little waist—or do you think I'm too fat? Maybe I could lose a little—and with maybe a *bustier* with a sheer overlay. And the skirt: with a train, okay? The longest fullest train to swish behind me as I descend the stairs—oh it doesn't matter what stairs, Swampy Jo! Lots of lace and flowers, my hair all up in something smooth and elegant. Maybe a single curl falling down one side just by my cheekbone. Oh yes. And Daddy," she coos, "Daddy can walk me down the aisle and give me away."

My tiredness moves in like a storm, making Aunt Cassie's pasta supper suddenly not worth the energy.

That's when I let it fly, about the idiocy of wedding traditions, of how preposterous it is for a father to 'give away' a daughter to her new husband, as if she were a piece of furniture. As if she ever 'belonged' to him in the first place. I stomp off quite dramatically, away from the steaming lasagna. For the first time I consider that perhaps Mr. Habbernashy was right to engage me in the Performing Arts in my one and only elective course.

Later, Aunt Cassie comes downstairs to find me digging out the crud under the toilet base with a nail file, comforting myself with Mom's peculiar homecoming ritual. I should be showering, I know, but I cannot muster the strength. But there is more on Aunt Cassie's mind than a kiss goodnight. Her posture is curved in the same burdened way Mom's was after we'd been put to bed, when she would hunch over her textbooks at the kitchen table, too tired even to yell at us as we got up for a drink, then a pee, to get a book, whatever. Looking back on it now, I wonder if what we were really doing was checking on Mom. To see if she was still there. To see if she was still breathing.

I get into bed as Aunt Cassie requests. After a long while, she begins to speak. I listen attentively so that she may be done quickly and I can finish off the night blissfully alone.

"Swampy Jo, I was thinking about what you said tonight at dinner. To Madison. About fathers giving their daughters away. I was thinking about you, and your dad."

Inside me I curse. Can't anyone see this is none of their business?

"I don't blame you for being angry." Aunt Cassie fiddles with her fingernails, cleaning away non-existent dirt. I do not want to hear this. Not tonight.

"Maybe we can talk about this tomorrow," I offer. "I'm too tired tonight, Aunt Cassie. And I have a test in the morning. I just need to sleep. Maybe tomorrow."

Aunt Cassie smiles softly, sadly. The back of her hand strokes my cheek.

"Your mother used to say that, Swampy, when she wanted to avoid something unpleasant. Even to our father, who was such a scary man. When he told her she deserved a spanking, she'd say: 'Maybe tomorrow,' and our father, who had been furious a moment before, would throw back his head and laugh. She always got away with it. Some people have a knack for escaping unpleasantness."

I wonder if that's what Mom is doing now, in her hospital bed with her face turned to the wall. Escaping unpleasantness.

That's when I feel it coming, like a demon headed for my throat: Aunt Cassie is unleashing something dreadful, something I cannot bear to know, even as every fibre of me strains toward this moment of truth.

And that's when I start screaming. I'm really not even angry, not inside. It's like the outside of me just loses it all of a sudden and flips out, even though inside I feel very calm, observing myself dispassionately like the viewer of a documentary. I note how my hands tremble, the rawness of my voice, which is much louder than necessary. The paleness of my legs, the blueness of veins bleeding through translucent skin, surprises me. Is that me, I think? Are those my limbs? I can see the inside of my face, my eye holes, like a mask I cannot control.

I say a lot of things, most of which don't make sense. Mr. Habbernashy must be having some effect on my style of speech: I start a sentence without finishing it, with many pauses and grunts of frustration thrown in. The gist of it is simple, when I finally get it out.

"My father would like me better if I were a boy. I am a mistake as a girl. He hates me because I'm not a boy!"

It is my defense against the worse things I can feel her needing to say. The threat rings through me, rattling my bones.

"He even named Joseph after me, in a way. Like my brother is some kind of improved carbon copy of me. Like I'm just a rough draft."

Aunt Cassie is shaking her head. Tears line her face like prison bars. This only makes me wilder. "No," she is saying, but I can barely hear her. My ears are blocked by the firestorm in me.

"Swampy Jo, you are not a mistake! The problem is not that you're a girl. You've got it all wrong, Swampy Jo. The problem is with your father, not you!"

"But it is my problem if my dad has a problem with me!"

Aunt Cassie stops, dead. Her stillness shuts me down completely. We are in the eye of the storm. From inside my head, I look out through my eyeholes and wait. What is she going to say? I feel thunder coming.

A heavy sigh springs her to life.

"Swampy Jo," she blurts, "your father molested you when you were five."

The words hit the outside of me and bounce off.

"What?" I say. The words have not penetrated.

"Your father molested you when you were five. You told your mother. That's why she asked him to leave, the very day you told her what had happened."

The words bounce off my outside again, but some essence of them soaks through.

Immediately I am attached again, outside to inside.

"No," I say full voice. "You are wrong."

Aunt Cassie looks so sad. She shakes her head.

"Don't fight it, Swampy Jo. It's true." Her voice breaks.

"No," I say. "You're wrong. It's not true."

Nothing rattles inside me. I am solid as iron. Aunt Cassie crumples in the face of my strength, as though my confidence makes this all so much worse.

"Your mother was away," she explains, simplifying events as you would to a small child. I am shrinking as she speaks.

"Your father was with you and Joseph for the night; just one night. When your mother returned from her trip the next morning, you told her that your father touched you. You were very specific. You showed her on your doll where he touched you. There is no mistake, Swampy Jo. Your mother believed you. I believed your mother. She told your father to get out or she would call the police. Then she called me. She didn't want me to come over, she didn't want to make it worse for you. She needed to think, she said, about what to do next. There's no mistake, Swampy Jo. Your father sexually abused you."

Under the tremble in Aunt Cassie's voice, she is rock solid.

In my mind's eye I have shrunk to the size of my five-year-old self. I am on a search and rescue mission, excavating graves of memories for clues. Can any of this be true?

Full colour, live action images pop up in my brain like living index cards. Flipping through these memories, I find myself in the bath, giggling. It isn't Mom, but dad by the bath tub, which is in itself unusual. I have him all to myself. My Daddy. He is smiling at me in a funny, strained way, and he keeps looking away toward the nursery door, where Joseph is crying in the background, unhappy in his crib. Daddy's lips are pressed together in a straight line. *Hurry, hurry up*, he says. Splashing him with bubbles will make him laugh, I think. I am wrong. Abruptly, he stands me up in the tub, and scrubs me with a bar of soap in his bare hands, a little too hard. My neck, my arms, my belly, my bottom (front and back), all in a row down to my knees. His huge hands are hot and rough against my skin. *Bend your knees,* he commands. The bar of soap disappears between my legs. *Ouch Daddy,* I whine. *You're fine,* he says, moving the bar of soap to my thighs, then scrubbing the scabs off my knees. It hurts and tickles at the same time. My ankles and feet remain submerged in bath water, untouched. The rest of me is soap from head to toe: I am a standing totem pole of suds. One deep plunk in the bath water and the fun is over. I am not very happy. I squirm and sulk. The towel misses spots. Daddy cannot get my pyjamas on right, and he won't let me wear my favourite pair. I am stuffed into the ugly green ones with the cuffs that are too tight. All the while Joseph is crying. Stupid Joseph, I think; this is my Daddy, not yours.

The internal video chip plays on: I am asking for cookies before bed, as Mommy always allows, but Daddy yells instead of singing the cookie song. I go to bed fast. He doesn't kiss me.

In the next room, Daddy rocks Joseph softly, whispering *sh, sh, sh, my baby boy.*

My five-year-old middle burns with vengeance. The heat of it explodes through the top of my head, the tips of my toes. I am so angry, I am as big as my room.

In one fell swoop, my five-year-old self expands to become me again. I have run the video through my fourteen-year-old mind. There is nothing perverse here, nothing fearful. Only the monster of jealousy. I almost laugh, until the pain hits.

The scene that clicks into focus in my memory is terrifying. There is something over my eyes, something in my mouth. I am choking on it. It is everywhere, on top of me, I cannot get away. My hands, my feet are buried in it. It is in my nose, in my hair. I am disappearing in the foul blackness of it, swallowed up in the shame, the self-hatred, the guilt. *'Daddy is gone because of you,'* Mommy says, and I drown my despair in the worst, the scariest, most dangerous place I know: the mud bog on the beach.

But I don't get eaten alive, like I think I might. I survive.

"No, Aunt Cassie," I shake my head. "You must have it wrong. I don't remember anything like that. It couldn't have happened the way you say," but she does not hear what I mean.

"You were so very young, Swampy Jo. You must have blocked it out. That often happens when a child is faced with something so..." A ripple of disgust transforms Aunt Cassie's face. "Something so foul." A shadow of hatred burns in her eyes.

Her conviction broadsides me. Could it be true? Could something have happened during the night, something more than a fit of envy and a hurried bath? My confusion strikes Aunt Cassie as a triumph; she quickly regains her composure.

"It's hard to accept these things as real, Swampy. I know. It seems so unbelievable that the man who should be most respectful, most protective of you, could do so much harm. Could take, when he's supposed to be giving. But it does happen. In real life."

I sense a companionship with her that I do not understand.

She kisses me, on the forehead.

"You must not blame yourself, Swampy Jo. There is nothing wrong with you. You are perfect."

She wishes me goodnight, mounts the stairs, leaving me alone with my tangled thoughts.

How can I be perfect? Here is proof that I have ruined my family. We are homeless, fatherless, because of something I said when I was five. Can there be any truth to the accusation? Surely I would remember something so invasive. What could I have told Mom that would have convinced her that she had to turn out her husband, the father of her two children? That my Daddy had been mean, had scrubbed me hard up and down in a rushed bath, because his infant son was crying? Surely, there had to be more to it than that? What had Mom heard? What did I say?

The screen of my mind remains blank. There is something lacking, another piece of this puzzle. There must be more.

I cannot lie still, cannot settle at any cost. My mind is racing, my body pumped. Doing sit-ups on the hard concrete floor by my bed late into the night, my gut burns with the rhythm of the effort, and the question eats into me: What is missing? What am I missing? The tautness in my middle from all these stomach crunches feels good. The strenuous exercise causes my tissue to eat into itself. The hunger in my belly has me sharpened to a point. I feel larger than life, euphoric in the cloak of my pain. Like the compulsion that makes you fiddle with a sore tooth, I dive into the hurt eagerly. My stomach is tight to the point of snapping. With each abdominal curl, I demand of myself: why did dad leave? What did I say? What did Mom hear?

The answer taunts me, just out of reach. But the perfect truth is here inside me, buried beneath layers and layers of imperfection, I feel sure of it. I will strip them away, and the certainty I need will be there, waiting right in the middle of me, where I left it when I was five years old.

And then there are my hands—my Mystic Cross hands. Surely my hands know something. My hands will lead me somewhere. Perhaps into Paul's arms?

A fog of need—for sleep, for food, for love—traps me in this illusion of purpose that is only a mirage. But I do not know this, not then. I feel only the thrill of my power over myself.

That night, by two a.m., I have begun to erase myself.

***

Madison is wailing, really and truly wailing. Her little pointed kitten face is puffy, blotched; it makes even her hair look bad, her clothes look wrong. What a fragile picture beauty is: when one element crumbles, the rest goes with it. Madison is worse than plain right now; she is downright ugly.

"He's cheating on me!"

Her mouth is all twisted. She is a waterfall of grief, streams running from her eyes, her nose, down her cheeks, dripping onto Aunt Cassie's kitchen table.

"Now, come on, Madison. You don't know that," Aunt Cassie soothes, wiping tears off the tabletop as quickly as they fall.

"Oh yes I do!" Madison shrieks. "Pockets is seeing someone else! I know it! There is no other explanation."

The world is ending, right here in Aunt Cassie's kitchen.

I am trying not to laugh.

The full story comes out in a wet, sloppy way. Paul isn't coming around much anymore; Madison hardly sees him. When she does, he can only concentrate his attention on her for a short while.

"He actually walks away halfway through a conversation. Right when I'm in the middle of saying something! He just says 'sorry' in this vague way and he leaves! He doesn't even explain or make excuses to cover his ass. Oh God!"

Another wail. Madison is not one to suffer in silence.

"Pockets isn't any fun anymore," she whines. "All he wants to do is sit in the park—and it's the middle of winter, for cripes sake—and all he wants to do is..."

I feel sure she is going to say "drink" or "smoke" or something worse, but she just stops right there. (Another apostle of the Mr. Habbernashy school of elocution?) I suppose there are some things even Madison is reluctant to share with Aunt Cassie. After all, Paul is underage for drinking, and Aunt Cassie does not approve of law breaking. I am oddly relieved to see Madison using some discretion.

Then out of nowhere she blurts it out, right there, onto the bare kitchen table.

"He doesn't want to fool around anymore!" Madison wails. "It used to be *all* he wanted to do. Now, he *can't*. He *has* to be doing it with someone else! It can't be a problem with *me*!" Madison's screeches fill the small room, bouncing off all the hard clean kitchen surfaces.

The slightest flicker of revulsion ripples through Aunt Cassie, a kind of gag reflex. Nonetheless, she taps Madison's hand affectionately.

"Now, now, Madison, of course it's not you. These things happen sometimes, you know. He is kind of young for that to be a problem, but still. It proves nothing. You know Paul adores you!"

Madison wails some more, which is becoming tiresome. A horrible, intimate image of Paul's naked, failing self clings to the table like a perverse centrepiece.

"Madison," I say, my voice razor-edged. "You knew Pockets was a player. You said it yourself."

My words slap her full in the face. Her ugly soggy features stretch into an open-mouthed gasp:

"It's you, isn't it Swampy? He's cheating on me with you!"

At the moment she cannot see how preposterous an idea this is. Aunt Cassie assures her of the absolute impossibility of such a thing.

"Oh, come on now, Madison!" Aunt Cassie chides. "You know Paul wouldn't go for someone like Swampy Jo!"

Family, I see, is always ready to come to my defense, no matter how much it hurts.

Madison turns on her.

"You!" she hurls. "Mother, you told Pockets to go for Swampy Jo!"

Aunt Cassie is shocked.

"Madison, I did no such thing."

"Yes, you did," Madison spits, "you told him she was special, because of that palm reading crap. You made her look good to him. You made him think they somehow matched! Gawd, I don't know why I didn't see this coming. I mean, their names are all over the park. Jeezus! People have been talking about it practically since school started, but who cares, right? If some scuzzball wants to scrawl her name all over everything like some lovesick calf, then let her make a fool of herself. It's not like Swampy Jo is any kind of threat to me. No one thought it meant anything. But now, I know something's going on. Now it's embarrassing. I'm with Pockets. Do you know how this makes me look?"

"What did you say? What names?" I'm lost.

"Don't play dumb, Swampy Jo. Your name is with his, painted all over the park. Everyone's seen it. Why did you do that? Are you sick?" Madison is wild with fury.

"But I didn't, I..."

"Well if you didn't, then he did!"

"But Madison, why would Paul do that? He's been dating you." Aunt Cassie squints, trying to understand.

"Well, somebody did it!" Madison screeches. "You've ruined everything, both of you! I hate you!"

In one rapid-fire sweep, she thrusts away from the table, stomps off loudly to slam her bedroom door. Hard.

Aunt Cassie does not give me one of those looks that say 'how could you.' Her eyes are locked on the imaginary centrepiece we both see, of Paul lying bared to the world on her table. She must be seeing things from a different perspective than mine, however, because she sighs:

"Well, that's too bad. Paul is such a nice young man. I suppose Madison's heart is broken. A first love is always the worst. First loves are always disappointing. Of course, it could be worse, couldn't it, Swampy Jo?"

Her hand is on my shoulder in a conspiratorial way, as if we shared a common past. The same disgusted shudder that passed unintentionally through her runs the length of my spine, as though she's handed the feeling off to me in a revulsion relay.

Aunt Cassie leaves the room quietly, so that I am alone at the very clean kitchen table staring blindly at an image that isn't there, feeling somehow that all this is my fault. My head is spinning: who could have written our names in the park? Could Paul have done it? And then my heart begins to skip at what this might mean. Inside me, a voice I recognize as my own whispers: *there is something wrong here, some piece of missing information.* But I cannot think what it might be.

***

It is the second day of winter break. The endless school-less days stretch out barren before me. Aunt Cassie adds Yuletide dressings to her house as each day goes by. To escape the depressing Christmas cheer, I spend much of my day at the hospital. It is a cold brisk ten minutes' walk from Aunt Cassie's, along the steel footbridge over the rail yard, along the tree-lined streets stripped of life now, alongside the frozen lake. The hospital nestles on a hillside edge of the park, with the Psych Unit rooms facing the water. A nice picture of freedom, I muse, for the institutionalized.

Mom is in a private room now, on dad's instructions. Visits with her are a lot like being alone. Still unmoving, she glares at the pallid landscape on the other side of the window. Only her breathing changes on occasion, from shallow sleep rhythms to laboured wakeful breaths. It is painful to watch.

"I'm sorry, Mom," I whisper, afraid to say it aloud. "Isn't a real person better than an angel?"

But I know the answer.

At first I spend my time poking about her room, then the adjoining bathroom (which I clean) then further spaces. Roving the stifling hallway I come across a gold mine: a storage closet packed with weigh scales. It takes me a moment to figure out how to adjust the weights along the horizontal bar to read my poundage. It takes time for the stick to quit bobbing. The first scale reads 105 pounds. The second says 100 even. The third is in between. Frustration squeezes me: the numbers should be dropping quicker than this. I'm hardly eating. Even the laxatives don't seem to be working. The solution is obvious: increase the amount of exercise I do.

Back in Mom's hospital room, I pass the hours on the frigid linoleum, doing crunches, push ups, leg lifts, squats. Only the occasional nurse appears, to check Mom's IV, her diaper, always with a cold smile for me. Very seldom will I hear dad approaching. The sound of him is unmistakable. From the moment he leaves the elevator down the hall, the thump of his heavy feet echoes through to me on the tile floor by Mom's bed. This alarm is always heeded: I scramble from the room, my athletic bag in tow, down the back stairs and out into the park outside.

A stretch of the lake is cleared for skating. It snakes along the shoreline in sweeping lines. Not many people use it regularly, making it even more attractive to me. The solitude presses in on me: nothing but wind, space, bitter biting cold. Perfection.

My skates laced, sports bag bound to my back, I hurl headlong down the ice trail, eager to raise my heart rate. I am not a skilled skater; the irregular ice surface worries me. Still, I pump my arms and legs as fast as I dare. It takes fifteen minutes for one lap. I cover two laps, then three. That's when I find Paul.

I must have seen him out of the corner of my eye. It is the only explanation. How else can I know the precise spot where Paul is hiding? At least it seems like he is hiding, tucked as he is, in among skeletal trees, his back to the frozen lake. One moment my skates slice along the ice surface, the next I am at a complete standstill, eyes riveted to the very place Paul is seated.

I do not bother to unlace my skates, using them instead to cut like guillotines into the snow beneath my feet. Paul never turns to look at me, though I have to circle him almost completely to reach the stand of trees in which he is cradled.

"Hello," he says.

His faint smile is not very convincing. He is sucking on a beer that he has taken from a hidden stash beneath the tangled roots of a towering elm. His hands are bare, the bottle frosted white with cold.

"Want one?" I decline.

"You'll freeze your hands," I say. "Take my scarf, and wrap your hand with it. You can get a burn from the cold, you know."

Paul smiles a lazy smile. He lifts a corner of the fuzzy purple scarf I have passed him, loops it around his neck.

"Soft," he murmurs.

The crystal air hangs between us, in danger of breaking, too fragile for words.

Finally, I say:

"Madison thinks you've found someone else."

Paul's reactions are slow. He takes a swig of beer, swallows it down with a kind of grimace. He looks at me, those warm brown eyes boring through the icy space between us. Another swig.

"No," he says simply.

I believe him. Out of his pocket comes a joint of some sort. I am not familiar with drugs of any kind, but I know enough to see it is not a tobacco cigarette. He lights it, offering it to me with a lifting of his eyebrows.

"No thanks."

Paul takes a long deep drag. The park, the lake, are empty, rendered mute by softly falling snow. This is a place for secrets.

"So," I ask, "is that why they call you Pockets? You keep drugs in your pockets?"

I wince at how naïve it sounds.

"Mm-hmm," he nods. "Always have a little something on me."

"Oh."

The trees overhead have branches like interwoven fingers, creating a shelter for us from the falling snow. Earth and sky fade behind a veil of sparkling flakes outside this intimate circle. I fancy that we enjoy the silence together.

Idle chatter is not my strength, nor is it Paul's, I deduce. So I utter something meant to be important and witty.

"Tell me where it hurts," I say in a manner intended to be playful. But my throat tightens and suddenly I want to cry.

Paul laughs, or imitates a laugh at least. Between swigs of beer and draws on the joint, he shakes his head. When his eyes hit me I can no longer tell where pupil and iris begin or end. His gaze is black and bottomless.

"I like sex," he says matter-of-factly. "It's the only time I can breathe right. The only time I can feel anything."

Another pull on the bottle, the cigarette.

"Here, I'll show you."

His voice would be malevolent if it weren't so devoid of drive. Still, his hands (bare even in this snow) reach for me, surprisingly warm under my coat. He pulls me to him; I don't think of resisting. His breath is hot on my neck. His hands are magic against my skin. I make a little sound of horror and of yearning, which makes him laugh his imitation laugh. My mouth is close to his, those deep red lips, but he does not kiss me. His mouth trolls across my face like a bottom feeder, a kind of fish in an aquarium scouting the invisible but very real walls of his prison. He presses me against him, hard, in a kind of desperate, angry tussle. My head is spinning with sensation.

Then he pushes me away.

For a moment the shame of rejection burns my face; I've been forced under, once again, into my childhood mud puddle. But then I catch his eyes and see that I am not the one who is drowning.

"You're too young, anyway," he says in a tone meant to be disdainful. "You're what: fourteen years old? Wouldn't want to go to jail, now would I?"

This last part is spoken in a sarcastic sing-song; he is speaking to someone absent, not to me.

"Your parents," I blurt, trying to get the conversation onto safer ground. "Are you going to be a lawyer like your parents?"

Paul snorts, shakes his head.

"Too dumb," he says. "I can barely read and write, at seventeen years old." He raises his beer. "It's my birthday today. Happy Birthday to me."

I acknowledge the day with well wishes.

"Thanks," he says. "My parents are happy too. Hell, when I got up today I found a present for me in the driveway, all wrapped up with a purple—sorry, that's a *mulberry*—bow. My very own car with a message written in lipstick—mulberry to match of course—'Happy Birthday, Son.' Very nice. Don't you think? 'Course, they were both gone to work by then. Didn't wake me up before they left. Didn't call. Didn't even use my name. Probably can't remember it. Just Happy Birthday, *Son*," he growls.

Blue shadows are growing at the bases of the trees, straining across the white expanse of parkland in an attempt to reach the darkening sky.

"Maybe you're dyslexic," I press, with too much enthusiasm. "Why you have trouble with reading and writing, I mean. Maybe you have some kind of undiagnosed learning disability. A lot of very intelligent people have learning problems."

Another snort on Paul's part.

"Nothing," he says, "is undiagnosed. All the diagnosises—or diagnosis-*ees*, or whatever the hell the effing word is. All the info is in. Believe me."

My tongue has more words ready, but Paul shuts me up.

"It doesn't matter, Swampy Jo. Or Sarah Jo, or whoever the hell you are. None of it matters. That's the difference between you and me, right there. Everything matters to you, and nothing matters to me. We have nothing in common."

The words, intended to sting, are able to do no more than imply anger. It is as though Paul hasn't the stamina for anything but mock emotion.

"We have the Mystic Cross in common," I say. I take off my mitt, place my pink palm against his fading one as proof.

He looks at our twin palms. Shrugs.

A sudden fear creeps up on me; the fibres, atoms and electrons of my being increase their frequency. The inside of me buzzes. It is that feeling again that something more, some unspeakable ghost is whispering around us.

"If you talk to Mr. Habbernashy," I say eagerly, "he can help. He has tests, to see if you do have a learning difficulty. You know Mr. H, the guidance counsellor at our school. He's ..."

Those dark eyes press into me once more. "Yeah. Hamsternasher. Right. He'll make it all better. Thanks for that. I'm on it." But his sarcasm has no bite. Paul leans back against a tree, perfectly at ease.

I force myself to calm down, to quit being so silly. *Look at him*, I say to myself, *this is not a big deal to him.*

After a moment, I ask "Why do you fool around so much? The sex, I mean." The word catches in my throat. "Aren't you afraid of diseases like AIDS?"

Paul shakes his head.

"I'm not gonna die a slow, quiet death like AIDS, with months and months of silent suffering. Not me."

"You don't know that," I counter.

Paul is unruffled.

"Some things you just know."

I am left to fill in the blanks: our talk is over. Paul tosses his bottle aside, buries his bare fingers in the snow as he rises.

"Bye," I call after him.

He barely lifts a hand in response, his thumb working on his mobile phone, the display bluer and colder than this winter day, like a shining window into nothingness. His footprints disappear in the sparkling, swirling snow. The heat of him now gone from our small circle, I am left shivering in the cold. The bare Mystic Cross in my mitt-less hand bleeds itching, red, criss-crossing slashes across the blue landscape of my palm. My mitten, back in place, cannot take the pain away.

It is when I am sliding down the knee-high wall near our grove that I see the patch of black stone where the snow has been knocked clear in an irregular circle. One swipe of my mitten clears the soft powdering of flakes on the surface. 'SWAMPY JOE,' it reads. Under it, in the same crude capitals, is 'POKETS.'

My eyes search the landscape for signs of Paul. The snow has already closed in around his footprints, leading me nowhere.

Chapter Five

Three days after Paul celebrates his seventeenth birthday, I turn fifteen. Aunt Cassie celebrates the occasion with an elaborately iced birthday cake, the kind that begins in a pouch, then (with the addition of eggs, water, and twenty minutes of oven heat) *pouf!* becomes a life size rendition of a home baked goody. Madison contributes by frosting the cake, licking the pre-packaged icing off her spatula with great relish, between swirls, making sure to spread whatever germs she carries onto every edge of the cake's surface.

Even the bubbles in the milk are repulsive to me. Lined up along the edges of my glass, they are like little globes of spit.

"I'm not very thirsty," I plead. "Maybe just some black tea, if you don't mind, Aunt Cassie."

"No cake for me, Mom," Madison chirps. "Wouldn't want to bulk up, now would I. You enjoy the cake, Swampy Jo."

I nibble the edges of a forkful, spreading the rest of my slice around my plate so it looks like I have eaten more than I have.

"Crazy sweet," I say.

"Oh come on, Swampy Jo," Aunt Cassie chides. "It's your birthday for heaven's sake. How often do you intend to turn fifteen? You and Madison are exactly the same age now."

Madison's neck snaps her head around with such vehemence that her ponytail slaps her clear across the face, like the tail of a horse swatting at flies.

"For, like, twenty minutes, maybe." Madison sounds angry. "I'll be sixteen in weeks. Days, practically!"

Aunt Cassie waves a hand. "Yes, yes, I just meant for now, you're peers..."

"If you think for one minute that I am in the same league as Swamp..."

"No need to get your knickers in a knot, sweetheart. This is Swampy Jo's day, not yours. And no one is making comparisons. You're each your own person. Your own young woman." Aunt Cassie smiles at me. She looks like she means it.

I smile back, fiddling with another bite. It is difficult to avoid swallowing the cake, with everyone watching. 'Everyone' means Aunt Cassie and Madison, Joseph (who is visiting for the day), and dad, who simply hovers darkly by the kitchen doorway, looking impatient. As foreboding as a bad omen.

"You could have at least insisted she shower," dad hisses, much too loudly. Aunt Cassie blushes, sputters, sparing me the work of feeling embarrassed.

I open a few gifts: a sweater, a scarf in yet another pretty berry colour (which makes me think of Mom, alone and immobile in a hospital room several cold blocks away), a book (something silly and overpriced). Thankfully the gathering is over soon: dad leaves with curt instructions to have Joseph ready at eight. Everyone except Joseph scatters, and he and I are left alone together.

I would not have thought a brother could be any comfort, but he is. No matter how stupidly Joseph acts, I find him surprisingly charming. By early evening we have been outside, digging unreliable tunnels in the snow. We have drunk hot chocolate with marshmallows, which I use to warm my freezing hands, then manage to spill accidentally-on-purpose so that I don't have to drink all those calories. We have danced to televised music videos, poking fun at the pop artists' too-short skirts and too-deep cleavage. If it weren't for the ordeal ahead of avoiding yet another meal, the afternoon would be perfect.

"Swampy Jo?" Joseph asks me during a lull in the action. We are lying on our backs on the rough carpet in our basement apartment, studying the deepening shadows on our living room ceiling, which Mom painted a vigorous Dijon mustard colour only days before her hospitalization.

"Swampy," he repeats, because I have not looked at him. Joseph will only speak if, first, he makes eye contact. He sits up, hovering above me, so that we can't help but lock gazes.

"Do you think Mom is going to die?" Joseph's face is all eyes, earnest and demanding.

My heart deflates until it is as flat as a pancake.

"I don't know," I say evasively.

"Do you think she's already dead?" he probes.

"Not on the outside," I say, maybe too harshly. To help, I touch his hand.

"She's still breathing, Yofus," I soothe. "Mom will be okay."

I make sure not to promise, though.

Joseph continues:

"Maybe she's dead but she just hasn't realized it yet. Like when you turn the power off to a fan, but the fan blades keep spinning around for a while."

"Because of the momentum," I say. "The blades keep moving because they *were* moving. The force of spinning is still behind them, and they keep going until the momentum runs out."

"Yeah," he says simply. "Or maybe," he says, his eyes shining with the thinnest veil of tears, "maybe she's in a comma."

"You mean a '*coma*', bonehead. A 'comma' is a punctuation mark, indicating a pause…"

"Well, Mom's in a kind of pause!" Joseph retorts in an effort to restore his nine-year-old dignity.

"Maybe," I say noncommittally. I don't want to fight.

Dinner is served late, at seven o'clock instead of five-thirty. I struggle over the meal, which is barbecued chicken wings, one of the easiest foods to leave half-eaten without it showing: simply separating the bones into separate lengths, even with most of the meat still attached, gives the impression of having consumed quite a bit. Unfortunately, chicken wings are one of my favourite foods. It takes great effort to wipe the sticky barbecue sauce from my finger tips onto my napkin, instead of sucking the sweet goo off. A consistent flow of saliva makes me feel hungrier after the meal than I was when I started.

When dad arrives at ten minutes past eight to pick up Joseph, he suggests that the three of us go up to see Mom for the last twenty minutes of visiting hours. We head off together, bundled against the winter wind.

Nothing has changed.

I am back at Aunt Cassie's by 8:35.

***

"I just fell asleep, Madison. That's all. Chill," Paul is saying. He looks thoroughly relaxed, sitting back into Aunt Cassie's living room couch. This is one of his occasional appearances over this Christmas school break; his visits are always unannounced and brief. Each time, Madison rushes to meet him, drooling at his feet like a small puppy.

Tonight his usually tight T-shirt is barely stretched over his lean torso; he is thinner than I remember. With his arm over the back of the sofa, his legs splayed out in a relaxed fashion in front of him, he looks like a string marionette adopting a pose.

Madison erupts:

"Yeah, well, Pockets!" she blurts. "You can't fall asleep in a car with the motor running, parked inside a garage. Haven't you ever heard of carbon monoxide poisoning? Or is it carbon dioxide? *Die*-oxide. You see what I'm saying?"

Paul shrugs. His eyes are more hooded than ever, as if the effort required to open them is barely worth making.

"Maybe I had a bit too much to drink," he smirks.

Then you shouldn't have been driving, I think, but I don't say it aloud. I am eavesdropping from my place in the kitchen, where I am refilling my water bottle.

For some reason beyond my understanding, Madison finds Paul's explanation amusing.

"You nut," she teases. She is sitting very close to him, her long limbs woven in among his on the couch. "You're such a wild man. You never know when to pull back. Really, Pockets, you could've died. Everybody knows that if you fall asleep in a parked car, in a closed garage, with the motor running, there's a good chance you won't be waking up. Ever. If one of your buddies hadn't shown up and dragged you out of there, you'd have woken up *dead*."

In spite of her reprimands, Madison seems tickled pink by Paul's idiocy.

"Next time, turn off the car before you take a nap," she finishes with a giggle.

Paul smiles vaguely, nods.

In the kitchen, I am feeling that freaked out feeling that sneaks up on me more and more often now. My head seems to not be a part of my body, and something in my chest reverberates to an off-beat rhythm. Too much adrenaline, I reason, from today's exercise. I have just returned from an hour-long jog in the park; outside, my breath hung like storm clouds ahead of me, the cold gluing my nostrils closed. It had been hard going through the snow, but I made it. Now, here in Aunt Cassie's kitchen, I realize how tired I am. Biting back the urge to yell, I draw eagerly from my water bottle like a hungry infant: water, I've read, helps to flush out adrenaline.

From where he sits in the adjoining living room, Paul blinks at me, but quickly loses interest; he returns his vacant gaze to the hyper television set. The pocket of his jacket bleeps, which he ignores. Beside him, her empty head on his hollow chest, Madison sighs happily.

***

On the first day back at school in January, Mr. Habbernashy corners me in his cramped little office during lunch period. No niceties first, not this time. Mr. H goes straight for the jugular.

"How much do you weigh, Sarah Jo?" He uses his most authoritative voice. I note with some surprise that he is the only person I know who cannot intimidate me.

"I don't know," I say in a vague way, as though the thought has never occurred to me. Mr. Habbernashy is not taken in by my nonchalance. Rightly so: I know that I weigh exactly eighty-three pounds; a quarter pound under, in fact.

Mr. H sputters.

"Now come on, Sarah Jo. I've got eyes in my head and they're pointed at you. I've noticed you've lost some weight since September. Weight that you didn't need to lose."

A glance at Mr. H's portly frame tells me he should hardly be the judge of that.

"Now, I'm worried about you, Sarah Jo," Mr. H rambles. "How many pounds have you dropped?"

When I don't respond, Mr. H ruminates.

"I'd say you've lost twenty pounds," he guesses. "At least that much, maybe as much as twenty-five pounds."

He might as well have criticized me, the way his comment stings. I have, in fact, lost a fraction over twenty-nine pounds. Almost thirty. I am appalled that he cannot tell.

No one cares about me, I think. *This just proves it. If anyone cared they would know how much I've lost.*

But I say nothing.

My back is very straight in my chair, my attention complete. I know how to be a good student, how to listen when the teacher is talking. Mr. H barrels ahead.

"You know, Sarah Joanne, those baggy clothes you wear don't fool me. I know you've been dieting, and I know you're doing this on purpose—losing weight I mean." Mr. H looks sadder than I've ever seen him look. His troll face is a mess of ruts and valleys as his face and forehead collapse into a frown.

"There's a name for what I think you're doing, Sarah Joanne," he says gently. "Anorexia Nervosa. An eating disorder."

I am so proud I want to scream. Not of Mr. Habbernashy for figuring it out, but of me. This feels like a celebration to me. All these months, I've been exercising not only my body but my will, which is now bulging with power. Power over myself. And power over Mr. H's peace of mind, it seems. But I don't want to care about that.

Mr. Habbernashy's face is buried in furrows.

"This is very serious, Sarah Jo. Life-threatening, in fact. To have lost the weight you have, so much, so quickly, you must be starving yourself."

His voice is very quiet, his eyes intense.

"Sarah Jo, are you still getting your period? Anorexics stop menstruating when their weight and body fat levels drop too low."

Oh god, I think.

I've not had a period in three months. Something big—like pride—pushes through me, up into my chest, my throat, pushing up the corners of my mouth.

Mr. H sighs and frowns, his eyes almost disappearing in the tangle of wrinkles that result.

"Sarah Jo," he pleads, "if you restrict your food intake like this, you miss an essential growing period. You may not gain your full height."

I almost laugh. *So what?* I think defiantly. *Being short has its advantages.*

"You won't build the bone mass you'll need."

I will always be thin, I think, *so I don't need thick bones.*

"There's no getting that back. Starvation is hard on your body, Sarah Joanne. You're hurting yourself."

Mr. H's miniscule eyes shine like marbles.

"You're hurting your heart, Sarah Jo. Starvation messes up your heart rhythm. You can suffer complete heart failure."

He is wrong, of course.

"People die from this, Sarah Jo."

Mr. Habbernashy's voice quivers. I am not budging.

After a long pause, he tries a different tack, like an expert sailor navigating into a shifting wind.

"I've read up on this, Sarah Joanne, and learned that certain behaviors are typical of anorexics," Mr. H says matter-of-factly. "Do any of these sound familiar? Obsession with weight. Non-stop exercise. Preoccupation with food. Distorted view of one's appearance: 'seeing' fat where there isn't any. Elaborate schemes for avoiding eating: shuffling food around, cutting it up in little tiny pieces, hiding it, pretending not to be hungry, making excuses not to eat. Counting bites, eating only in certain positions, certain locations, with certain dishes or cutlery. Vomiting after eating, even the smallest amounts. Using laxatives ..."

He must register a spark of recognition in me, because his voice takes off with renewed zeal.

"Setting rules—games—around eating. Eating everything with chop sticks, or with a baby spoon. Eating only green things on Mondays, Wednesdays and Fridays, then only orange foods the rest of the week: that kind of thing? Not being able to sleep or rest or sit, without getting up to exercise."

It's getting so hard to sit still.

"Not being able to think of anything else. Does it take all your energy to keep this up, to get your weight lower and lower? All that energy spent on self-denial?"

Mr. H is relentless. He looks at me squarely, his hands on the arms of his chair. His face almost expressionless.

"If someone were doing this to you, persecuting you, starving you and working you to the bone, I would stop them." His cheek trembles, as if he might break apart. "I would have to do everything I could to try to stop them."

Mr. H's pudding face moves, his jaw shifting.

"Is this a silent scream for attention? Maybe it is. After all, we all need some attention."

I listen to my breathing: shallow, quick. *Please finish,* I think, *please finish now, Mr. H, I have to go*. But I keep my mouth shut.

"Sarah Jo, has anyone told you lately what a fine girl you are? That they loved you?"

I fidget as though a snake has just crawled up my back, but I remain silent.

"But," Mr. H offers, "this self-starvation of yours..."

He leans in, getting personal.

"...is it a way to control your feelings by choking them off? A way to swallow up anger and anxiety, if there's no safe place for you to release it? Hostility turned inward? Or a desire to... actually... disappear?"

Mr. H's nose is very close to mine now. He is searching the map of my face for an answer. I am not obliging.

Something in me tightens.

Mr. H sighs and sits back. "Some experts think that anorexics want to return to childhood, to escape the overwhelming world of sexuality. Does that make sense to you?"

Hostility is growing in me like wildfire.

Mr. H grabs both arm rests of his chair again, preparing for the Big Statement. I stiffen my back for the attack.

"Sarah Joanne," he begins slowly. "Some psychiatrists think that an eating disorder like this may be a result of—well, of a sexual trauma. Sexual abuse."

I don't like where this is going.

"And, I've noticed another thing, something distinctive about you. If you are anorexic—and I am afraid that you may be, Sarah Jo—well, one piece doesn't fit the pattern. Most anorexics are meticulous about their personal appearance, just as they are about their work, their eating patterns, their exercising. They spend hours grooming. You ... well, your poor hygiene—not washing, not combing your hair or brushing your teeth—this is common in people who've suffered sexual abuse. It's a kind of ... protection, maybe, from more unwelcome sexual attention, or a kind of retaliation perhaps. Or just another act of self-loathing."

There is a question rising in his voice. I feel it coming.

Mr. H is as gentle as can be, his eyes lost in his worry lines.

"Sarah Jo, have you been sexually abused?"

Bile rises in my throat.

"No," I say angrily.

***

I do not return to my classes that afternoon. Instead, for the first time in my life, I play hooky. It is a very long walk from the high school to the park, the hospital. I cut through the rail yard to shorten the trek, being careful to stay clear of the tracks as much as I can. Men in the distance are hitching and unhitching rail cars, which come together—CLANG!—with a piercing clap like thunder. All at once, a great holler rises from the opposite side of a line of box cars. Workmen scramble from their tasks to the spot where the scream arose. Even from this distance I can hear the rough male voices hurling swears, though only snippets of their conversation are clear:

"...you son-of-a...gonna get yourself mangled!"

"...dangerous...lucky you didn't lose your legs...!"

"...crazy idiot kids...!"

Suddenly from between two box cars, a gangly dark haired figure is thrust away from the train tracks and onto the ground by a burly, cursing form.

"You're trespassing!...insurance won't cover some lunatic getting smashed between two cars...lose my bloody job over this!...Stay out!"

The herculean man departs, arms flailing and mouth rumbling with profanity. The dark figure splayed on the dirt-packed snow between the rails rises, skinny as a stick in his open leather jacket; he bends at the waist, hands on his knees, and chuckles. Paul. I know the curve of his body on sight, by some gut instinct. There is no one else around him, no buddies to show off for: this dare is for himself alone. He has not seen me.

"Stupid ass," I shout, but the colliding box cars swallow my sound. "One of these days you'll get yourself killed!"

I keep walking. I am too wrapped up in my own escape from Mr. Habbernashy to waste effort on him. Paul has left the railway flats and is climbing a nearby hillside heading for downtown by the time I reach the area under the steel footbridge. Within minutes I am in the park, then the hospital, then Mom's hospital room. I fully expect to find Mom in her hibernation pose: eyes open, averted, body crumpled into the bedcovers. What I don't expect is to find dad by her bedside.

Crying.

I do not enter, preferring the biting cold outside.

I look at my hands a long time that night. I look for meaning between the lines. I look for the mystery of me, and of Paul, spelled out for me. I look for something to make sense.

***

“I just think a bit of churching would be good for you, Swampy Jo, that’s all.”

Aunt Cassie is dressed to the nines, blotting her thick red lipstick with a tissue. She keeps glancing at the plastic cross of Jesus bleeding above her kitchen table.

“Is unc’ coming?”

The tissue in Aunt Cassie’s hand looks like it has mopped up a nosebleed, it’s so saturated with red.

“Unh-uh. He’s headed out again. He’ll be gone two weeks. Big international trade show.”

I blow my bangs up from my face.

“What?” Aunt Cassie asks.

“Nothing,” I lie.

She puts her hands on her hips, the red tissue suffering in one fist.

“It’s just that I never see him,” I say. “He’s like some kind of ghost. He comes and goes, I hear his footsteps up here sometimes, or his voice, so he must exist…”

“Of course he exists!”

“…but I never see him. It’s just…weird. Don’t you get lonely for him, Aunt Cassie?”

She turns to the mirror by the door and blots some more. The tissue begins to disintegrate. “Ah,” she says, a short, irritated sound, and she waves the crumbling tissue like a flag of surrender. “We need to go now, Swampy, if we’re going to make the service. If we head out right this moment we won’t be late. There won’t be much parking left. Get your coat, please.”

"What about Madison? Is she going?" I ask.

Aunt Cassie shakes her head. "No." She stuffs the wad of dead tissue in the pocket of her light blue wool pea-coat.

From the crack of her bedroom door, Madison fires a one-eyeball torch at me. A crinkled eyeball: Madison is smiling.

Well, that's it then.

"Why the sudden interest in church, Aunt Cassie? Mom hasn't taken us in years."

The door is open now. Cold pushes in like bad news.

"Maybe a little faith is what we all need. We can pray for your mom while we're there. Maybe that will work."

The car ride is short, over the overpass and up a hill, toward another, smaller inner-city lake. We park across the street and around a corner from a plain brick building set at an interesting angle on a patch of graying snow.

"So this is for Mom," I say, looking to Aunt Cassie for confirmation. Her dark hair and bright lipstick pop against the snowscape.

"It can't do any harm," she says.

Her stride is long and confident in heeled boots, but her eyes look wary. She keeps her head at an angle to the church structure, like a cop entering a gun fight. She holds one clenched hand high in front of her chest, the other fist cocked daintily at her side, hidden in a light blue leather glove.

Inside, rows of well-dressed people speak in hushed tones. We move to the front pews, along the margins of the room.

"Holy crap, Aunt Cassie, what is that?" I can't help ducking a little.

Above us, hooked to massive cabling hanging from the vaulted ceiling, a ten foot mannequin of Jesus stares down at us, eerily elated.

"That's really creepy. How'd they get him up there?"

"Swampy! Shhhh!" she says, bowing her head and not looking at me. She smiles prettily at a grumpy woman sitting near the end of a nearly empty pew. The woman frowns, looks me over, and begrudgingly slides her ample backside along the wooden bench until there's room for Aunt Cassie and me to sit.

"Kneel first, Swampy Jo."

"Oh. Yeah, right. Almost forgot."

We kneel and Aunt Cassie seems to be praying. I can't take my eyes off the Jesus mannequin looming overhead. The length of his oversize body is strung out horizontally, ten or fifteen feet above the floor. Like his body is a mothership, docked and waiting to re-absorb its pods.

The grumpy woman hands us a hymn book, and a folded paper bulletin. An organ squawks to life, and a procession of gowned males parade down the centre aisle of the building, under the hovering Jesus above. The leader carries a cross twice his size, and I wonder if it will poke Jesus in the gut as the group makes its way to the altar.

The last man in the procession, who is cloaked in brighter colours than the rest, begins to speak. His words are friendly but his face is impassive. The crowd responds in unison, then repeats the outburst a few more times, with the priest's words providing lyrics to the crowd's monotone refrain. Then a flourish of hands all around us, drawing hurried crosses in the air, and we all sit.

Aunt Cassie's gloves are off, but her fists remain clenched.

A man in a suit and tie mounts a podium, and begins to read. His deep voice resonates with drama, the words ringing out with ease.

"New Testament, the gospel of Luke, Chapter 23, verses 28 to 30. 'But Jesus turning unto them said, Daughters of

Jerusalem...,'" he reads, "'...weep not for me, but weep for yourselves, and for your children. For, behold, the days are coming, in which they shall say, Blessed are the barren, and the wombs that never bare, and the paps which never gave suck...'"

"What did he say, Aunt Cass? What are paps?" I try hard to whisper.

Aunt Cassie rattles one hand at me. Her eyes remain on the man at the podium. She looks frightened, or angry. Her red lipstick has begun to bleed into fine lines around her pursed mouth.

The grumpy woman beside Aunt Cassie leans her bulk forward, one arm reaching across Aunt Cassie to stab a finger at the folded program in my hand. The words are printed there.

I nod a thank you, and she retreats.

"'...Then shall they begin to say to the mountains, Fall on us, and to the hills, Cover us.'"

The suited man's voice hangs in the air like a vision in words. Jesus looms above, smiling approvingly.

Say to the mountains, Fall on us, and to the hills, Cover us, I repeat to myself, reading the pamphlet. *Wow.*

"Our Father who art in heaven," the priest begins, and the crowd joins in, heads bowed, voices bored.

After a little more formal talking, the ceremony builds to communion. Young children dressed in white robes hand small silver dishes to the priest, bowing. "Father, Father, Father," they whisper. The priest holds up a circle of bread the size of a man's head, then a silver cup to the sky, where the large Jesus figure floats, and a small bell tinkles magically from behind the altar. People start to line up in quiet, orderly rows, each pew-full standing and waiting their turn to step up to the priest, who holds a gleaming chalice from which he takes a perfect white circle and holds it up to the light before handing it to each member of the congregation, who one by one tuck it in their mouths and step aside.

Overhead, the mannequin Jesus smiles, his eyes too wide, his hand raised in a sign of welcome. He looks like he is swimming up there, and we are minnows in water below him.

"Snorkeling Jesus," I whisper to myself.

When our pew rises, the grumpy woman shifts her weight toward the centre aisle, to join the communal line. Aunt Cassie blocks my way.

"Out," she points.

The sun is bright outside, too bright. I have to squint to see the walkway.

"Wha...? Did I do something wrong, Aunt Cass? I was just...that Jesus statue...I mean...I wasn't being rude, really, I've just never seen..."

"It wasn't you, Swampy. Really. I needed to get out of there."

The red tissue from Aunt Cassie's pocket has reappeared in one blue-gloved fist, where it is being squeezed smaller and smaller with never-ending pinches.

"All that 'our Father,' 'my Father,' 'give thanks to the Father' stuff, I just couldn't breathe."

By the time we reach the car, Aunt Cassie has slowed down. She straightens up and lets the depleted tissue fall to the ground in a sprinkle of red and white. She looks up at the sky, which is blue and cloudless.

"Well, enough of that," she says, and rubs her blue coat against her flanks. "How 'bout a cappucino, then?"

"Um," I say.

"Hot chocolate. Whatever. Caffeine. Something! I'm sorry I got you out of bed for this, Swampy. It was a thought. But I can't. Can't do this particular thing, any more. Not for me. Nope."

She dusts her blue coat off again. Her bright lipstick is fading into the real colour of her lips.

"Okay," I say. "Coffee's good. Tea, maybe?"

There are no calories in tea.

She nods.

"Get in."

Back at Aunt Cassie's, the bleeding plastic cross comes down and gets stuffed in a drawer with kitchen linens until after supper, when it goes up again.

Later, back in my basement home, I look up the passage from the church bulletin, in the bible mom keeps in her bedside drawer. The white paperback volume lies open on the hard floor in front of me. The pages, as transparent as tissue paper, whisper between my fingers as I thumb through them. It takes me awhile to find it:

New Testament, the gospel of Luke, Chapter 23, verses 28 to 30. The wording is different from the more formal wording in the folded church program, but I recognize it immediately.

"Women of Jerusalem!...," it says, "...Don't cry for me, but for yourselves and your children. For the days are coming when people will say, 'How lucky are the women who never had children, who never bore babies, who never nursed them!' That will be the time when people will say to the mountains, 'Fall on us!' and to the hills, 'Hide us!'"

I sit in the growing darkness of my basement apartment, and wonder what this means.

I wonder about this unhappy time when women without children are considered lucky. Better off, more desirable: blessed. When women are cherished for their flat bellies and perfect breasts: for having the bodies of childless women. And the punishment is that everyone (not just the women and children, but everyone) would wish the mountains would fall on them, that the hills would hide them, would cover them up.

I wonder about Mom, far away from me, but still my mom. I wonder if she's sorry she had me, and Joseph. I wonder if she wishes she'd never married my dad, and given birth to our family. I wonder if she wishes the mountains would fall on her, and that the hills would cover her up.

I wonder if I do.

I sit in the underground space my mother has found for us, alone, without her or anyone, and I wonder.

Chapter Six

It comes as a shock when Paul asks for me at Aunt Cassie's door one dark February night. It is ten o'clock, too late to go out for a walk in the park.

"Go," Aunt Cassie urges, pushing me toward the door.

Out of the corner of my eye, I see Madison at the end of the hall, staring us down until the very moment the front door clicks shut.

Outside, the winter wind howls off the lake, moaning around us like a herd of ghosts. We must speak very loudly, our heads pressed close together, in order to understand one another.

"I wanted you to know I think you're great," Paul says.

"What?" I strain to hear.

"I said you're great!" Paul hollers. "Really. No matter what anyone else might think or say. You've got something other people don't."

I cannot believe my ears; surely the wind has fooled me. This is so out of character for Paul. No one ever tells me things like this. I must have misunderstood.

"You mean, that I care too much about every little thing," I respond defensively.

"No. Well, yes," Paul shouts. "It's not a bad thing to care. You're very special, Swampy Jo. I thought you should know that."

Thankfully, the wind fills the gaps in our conversation, because I don't know how to take this. It's hard walking through the snow; icy spray off the banks hits us in the face, pinching. Under each footstep the hard surface crust gives way, so that we are trudging up the hillside in knee-deep drifts. Finally we reach the top of the crest, where the gazebo sits on the edge of an outcropping of rock, facing the frozen lake. Beads of light zigzag across the ice surface: the headlights of snowmobiles, their riders enjoying the last bit of safe riding that the season will allow on the frozen lake.

"It will be spring soon," I say to fill the awkward silence. Inside the shelter of the gazebo, there is no longer any need to shout. "It's hard to believe that in another few weeks, the ice on the lake will begin to melt, and the snow will be gone. Things can change so fast."

"I guess," Paul says, not really listening. He stares out at the palettes of blues, mauves and navies that make up the sky, the trees, the snow. His eyes chase the dots of light playing like fireflies over the frozen lake.

"You should button up your jacket," I say, noticing the flimsy T-shirt he wears beneath his coat. His hands and head are bare, but around his neck is my fuzzy mauve scarf. "Aren't you cold?"

"I suppose," is all he says.

Another long silence. I venture a question.

"Why did you come to get me tonight, Paul?"

He is slow to respond, considering his words. Something hopeful springs up in me.

"Did you ... Paul, did you write that thing in the park? Our names ..."

He shakes his head in confusion. "What? Oh. Right. Our names in the park." He laughs. "This isn't about that. I'm taking a car trip," he says. "To Niagara Falls, I think. I'm leaving tonight."

"But spring break isn't for three or four weeks yet. You can't just cut school, Paul."

He smiles at me.

"Yes, you can, Swampy Jo."

"Not without affecting your marks. Paul, if you don't quit goofing off, you might fail your year again ..."

Paul waves my words off with a sigh.

"You follow the rules, Swampy Jo. It seems to be your thing. And maybe it's a good thing. At least then you know when you're screwing up. But rules aren't my thing. I'm going on a car trip, in my new car. I just wanted to say goodbye to you before I go, to tell you I think you're a good kid. You'll be alright. You're smart, and you're not half as bad looking as you think you are. Not everybody could wear an orange wool knit hat and red gloves like that," he says, smirking at my cap and mitts, "and pull it off with such style."

"Don't tease me, Paul," I say with more irritation than I intend.

"Really, orange hat aside, Swampy Jo, I'm not teasing. You've got your own way. You're ... cute. A bit scrawny, maybe, but you'll fill out ..."

"Look who's talking!" I pounce. "You're getting skinnier every day!"

He seems embarrassed for a moment.

"Yeah," he says with real concern. "I just can't seem to keep any weight on. Anyway, it doesn't matter. We were talking about you. You've got a lot on the ball. You see things ..."

His voice trails off: this is becoming too much like work.

"I just wanted you to know before I go," he finishes.

A hard nugget of anger inside me flares into an illogical rage.

"You don't care about me," I stammer.

"I do, Swampy Jo. In a way, I even love you." Paul's voice is patient, almost sleepy.

"No you don't!" I rage. "How can you love me? You don't even know me!"

"You've been a friend to me," he says.

"I haven't been *anything* to you, Paul! What you're saying isn't making any sense ..."

He pulls the length of purple mohair from around his neck.

"And I wanted to give you back your scarf," he says calmly, placing it in my hand. "Thanks for lending it to me."

"No, it's yours now, Paul. You can keep it." An overwhelming desire to have him keep the scarf takes over.

"I don't need it," Paul says simply.

A mixture of fury and panic rises in me, like a tidal wave out of nowhere. I am a girl possessed.

"You can't leave," I sputter.

"It's only a car trip, Swampy Jo," Paul soothes.

I don't know why I'm freaking out, but I am. I grab him, my arms around his neck, fumbling with the scarf.

"Keep the scarf, Paul. Please. You're never dressed warmly enough. You'll catch your death ..."

"I don't need it, Swampy," he repeats.

My mind is racing, my heart pumping wildly. Something is very wrong.

In an act of desperation, I press my cold lips against his. This is our—my—first kiss. Up on my toes, I push my mouth, my whole face, into Paul's, flattening our noses: more an act of aggression than of love.

Perhaps if he had pushed me away, I could have regained my composure again. But he just stands there, waiting, until I'm done.

"What's wrong with you!" I scream.

Already he is moving away from me, back into the darkness and the wind outside the gazebo. I can barely make out what he says.

"Bye, Swampy Jo. Remember that I care about you."

I am alone with my raging heart, my strange fear. By the time the wave of anxiety in me has crested, Paul is nowhere to be seen. I run all the way back to Aunt Cassie's through the quicksand drifts of snow.

Madison is waiting for me, sitting quietly in the darkened living room.

"So, where did Pockets take you?"

"The park."

"Why?"

"I don't know," I tell her truthfully. "He wanted to tell me that he thinks I'm okay."

"Did he tell you he loves you?" Madison fumes.

"Yes," I answer. She does not wait to hear the rest.

"I knew he was a player," she cries. "I'm such an idiot!"

"But Madison," I squeak, running after her. "There's nothing going on between us. I... I don't know why he said those things. It doesn't make sense. We don't even know each other."

"Pockets only wants to 'know' you in one way. He loves anyone who puts out for him," Madison howls.

"But Madison ... he and I never..."

"Don't lie to me! Pockets kissed me off today. He told me what a nice girl I am, how pretty I am, how much fun I am to be with. He told me he loved me. He loved me!" Madison is screeching now. "I should have known it was just a cover, a... kind of sick joke. He was kissing me off... in favour of—you!" The thought repulses her. "I guess it was Pockets who wrote your names together all over the park, after all. He must have had a thing for you from the start. Freak! I can't believe that he would choose you over me. That just proves what a loser he is. And you, Swampy Jo, you just stay away from me from now on. You don't belong here and you never will!" She slams her bedroom door.

Standing in the hall facing the closed door, I am searching for words to explain this whole misunderstanding to Madison. I hear the click of a lock, and realize that Aunt Cassie is standing in the entrance to her bedroom, as rumpled as her pyjamas.

"I heard," she says to me.

"But Aunt Cassie," I stammer, "it isn't like she says."

Aunt Cassie shakes her head.

"Just leave it, Swampy Jo," she whispers, closing her door.

All night long, I fight my restlessness with push ups, sit ups, leg lifts. It is impossible to sleep. At dawn, I add a layer to my clothing, then slip soundlessly out into the crisp winter morning. The streets, the steel footbridge, the stripped trees: all are hushed, unmoving. The park plays dead, buried in a carpet of dazzling white. The pressing silence breathes heavy secrets that I already know.

Finding the rock wall near our grove, I grope at the hard-packed snow, working little bits off the surface until I find our names, SWAMPY JOE, POKETS, like white bones on the hard black stone.

In a frozen calm, I wait.

Eventually, I don't know how much later, Aunt Cassie finds me.

"It's Paul, isn't it," I say. "He's been in an accident."

"Yes," she says, grief and confusion highlighting the lines in her face. "There's been a terrible car accident. They found him a couple of hours ago. Paul drove all night, and fell asleep at the wheel. How did you know?"

"I just did," I shrug.

Aunt Cassie heads back to the safety of her warm house. Out here, in the snow, the silence swallows me up.

***

"She's psychic," Aunt Cassie is saying. I can hear her talking to my uncle at the kitchen table overhead, if I stay very quiet in my bed in our basement apartment. In spite of her efforts to keep her voice hushed, the words drift down to me through the floorboards and the thin ceiling tiles.

"I mean it," she continues with a mixture of alarm and admiration. "You should have seen her in the park, just sitting there in the snow, confident as could be, waiting for me. 'It's Paul, right?' she said, even before I started to speak. It was unnerving!"

My uncle responds intermittently with a repertoire of noises to indicate agreement or disbelief, as he sees fit.

"Ooh," his deep masculine voice resonates through the floor, clearly doubtful.

"I don't care what you say," Aunt Cassie rebukes. "I know what I saw. What I heard. She just spit it out, cool as a cucumber: 'It's about Paul', she said. 'He's been in a car accident.' You know that Swampy Jo doesn't talk unless it's necessary, but it was all there in that one sentence. She knew Paul had been hurt. I don't know how she knew, but she did. I'd bet my life on it! I know she doesn't look the part, really—but maybe she does, after all. There's a certain gypsy quality about her, with those eyes that look right through you, the way she's always watching.

"And then there's that bit about their palms—the matching signs. The Mystic Cross. Maybe that's real, somehow."

My uncle's strong low voice joins hers in dubious, disinterested agreement.

I am buried on my mattress under layers of the thickest blankets from three beds—after all, Mom and Joseph are not using theirs. Beads of salty sweat spring up on my upper lip. I am not feverish; I have just been holding my legs out straight in front of me, several inches off the bed, in order to work my lower abdominal muscles. Constant exercise is the only way I can escape the spiral of fear inside me, which screws tighter each day. I feel the need to be ready, to be at my strongest, my leanest, as if at any moment the enemy (what enemy?) might force me to the test.

Sleep does not come easily for the nocturnal exerciser. Between bouts of isometrics, I drift into an exhausted slumber, marred by fitful dreams...

Paul is with me on the shores of the lake—our lake: my Mom and dad's, and Joseph's and mine. Paul and I are on our beach, by our big house opposite the park. From where we stand the distant park is lovely in its crystal cape of snow: as still as death. We are barefoot. The cold bleeds into my veins, my spine; I can barely move, the pain is so sharp. Paul is warm and happy; the cold causes him no discomfort. 'Let's swim,' he says, plunging into the frozen lake, which splinters like shards of frosted glass. Though I am frozen to the ground, my mind races—Paul is nowhere to be seen beneath the ice. 'Find him!' my mind screams, but my body cannot obey.

Then the spot of splintered glass into which Paul dove becomes an inky mass, black and thick, smelling of earth, bubbling up to spread like the flow of a gaping wound into the snow until it reaches my toes, swallows my ankles, my knees, my middle.

Suddenly I am sucked out of my body into the frozen sky above. I see that the icy earth has vomited black loam, a dark impenetrable puddle of dirt that is actually... Paul's... eye.

He smiles at me, his black eyes flat, as empty as a fresh black grave cut into the frozen ground...

I wake with a start, heart pounding. Just a dream, I mumble to myself, rolling over onto my belly, to lift my legs up straight behind me, working the muscles of my behind. I strain under the weight of all my many blankets.

***

The next morning, my feet take me directly to Mr. Habbernashy's office. A steaming coffee cup in his fat fist, Mr. H is startled to see me so early; he checks his watch with some confusion, to be sure he has not simply lost track of half a day.

"Sarah Jo," he beams. "Good morning."

My distress obvious, Mr. H ushers me to a seat and quickly adopts an appropriate pose behind his desk: he sets his coffee mug aside, plants his chin into the fertile hollow formed by his hands upon the desktop. He is fully and actively prepared to listen.

Unfortunately, I am not fully and actively prepared to make any sense. I try to find the right words. Any words. Mr. H waits. Like a caricature of a floppy faced puppy, his drooping wet eyes pleading, Mr. Habbernashy waits patiently for me to speak.

"So what if I'm psychic," I blurt, knowing how stupid the idea is, feeling twisted on the inside, fighting the urge to laugh hysterically.

Mr. H does not move, but his eyebrows climb high onto his forehead.

"Okay," he says simply, perfectly willing to play along.

I'm stuck for words again. Mr. H just looks at me. He looks and looks and looks.

"You said I was intuitive, remember? The Rorschach ink blots, the ... the handwriting analysis ... you said, you said I was highly observant, and ..."

"It's okay, Sarah Jo. Just keep breathing. Yes, yes, I said you were intuitive and highly observant. And that is what I see: a very observant young woman learning to trust her intuition, which, as far as I can tell, is a subconscious form of intelligence. The IQ tests and the ink blots, the Strong Interest Inventory—they're all theories of personality and intelligence. Different templates to measure yourself against."

"They're not true," I say. I say it like a statement, but it is really a question.

Mr. H shrugs. "I don't know," he says. "People argue about this and that, about what's valid, what's not. It's all a little all over the place." He laughs, but I can see that he doesn't want to hurt my feelings. "Whatever gets you thinking about yourself, about your strengths and your mysteries, about your potential ... well, that's a good-enough measure for me. Anything that gives you a sense of power and mastery over your circumstances ... well, how bad can that be? I don't think anyone, really, has any answers. Not real, dyed-in-the-wool, actual answers. Not answers that are across-the-board true."

Fudge, I think. And the bottom drops out of this new and hopeful world.

"But, still," I stammer. "Sometimes, I... know things."

"Yes," Mr. H nods. And I see he believes me.

So I tell him everything, in no particular order. About the palm-reading, the sign of the Mystic Cross found in my palm and Paul's. How Paul was happy the night he visited me, but I felt—no, I knew—that he was in danger. That when Aunt Cassie came to tell me about Paul's car accident, that morning in the park, I had been waiting for those very words, absolutely certain the news would come.

My hands shake in my lap; it is hard to sit still. Mr. H listens attentively, chin in his hands, until the story winds down. He prepares to respond.

"Maybe I'm crazy," I interrupt before he has a chance to speak. "Maybe it runs in the family." The image of my mother curled into a ball, face to the wall, springs to mind. "My Mom believes an angel did her dishes. If that's not crazy, what is?"

Mr. H tilts this way, then that. "Well," he begins.

"He has the same mark—Paul has the same Mystic Cross mark. In his hand." My palm comes up of its own accord. "Maybe that's how I knew."

Mr. H wiggles his nose, flares his nostrils like a bull ready to charge. In one swift movement, he sits up, he reaches into a drawer for a pamphlet, which he lays open on his desktop. After a long dark look at me, he begins:

"Sarah Joanne, I'd heard about the accident, which is bad enough in and of itself. But you've brought up something... else.

Tell me if any of these points apply to Paul Holditch, to what you feel about him."

He reads from the pamphlet:

"'Abrupt changes in personality.'"

I consider the point.

"Well, I haven't really known him that long," I stall.

Mr. H nods and continues.

"'Giving away prized or expensive possessions.'"

I think of my soft, fuzzy scarf, the one I'd given him to keep his hands warm that snowy day in the park, that he insisted on returning to me the night before the accident.

"Maybe. But he didn't give away his car. That would be his most expensive possession."

"Did the car mean very much to him?" Mr. H asks.

"No. He just thought it was another ploy on his parents' part to buy his affection. He didn't seem to care much about it. In fact, he barely used it. Except for the car trip he took, and then he—he crashed the car. Totalled it. The ambulance attendants, the cops, they had to pry him out with a ... a machine called the Jaws of Life ..."

Mr. H's voice snaps me back to the task at hand.

"'Increased use of drugs or alcohol,'" he continues.

I recall the beer stash beneath the roots of a tree in the park. Pockets full of ... what had he said? *'I always keep a little something on me.'*

"Probably."

"'Lack of self-esteem?'" inquires Mr. H.

'I'm so stupid,' Paul had said, *'I can barely read and write.'*

"Yes."

"'Drastic change in weight.'"

"Definitely," I say, remembering how he was suddenly so thin.

"'Unwillingness or inability to communicate.'" Mr. H plods on. "'Difficulty concentrating.'"

"Mm-hmm." *'He leaves the room right in the middle of a conversation,'* Madison had said.

"'Sexual promiscuity.'" Mr. H speaks clearly, no recrimination in his voice.

"Yes." *Paul, the player.*

"'Sexual difficulties.'"

I nod, my cheeks flushing as I recall Paul's hands on me, our bewildering, failed embrace beneath a grove of leafless trees one snowy afternoon; Paul, pulling away in embarrassment.

"I thought it was my fault," I whisper, cringing at the memory, then at the fact that I've spoken my shame aloud. Mr. H, for his part, ignores the acknowledgement and continues efficiently itemizing the pamphlet list.

"'Hostile or reckless behaviour?'"

Paul's games in the railway yard, jumping between colliding box cars. Paul falling asleep in a running vehicle, parked in a closed garage. Paul getting dangerously drunk.

"Yes." A new image of Paul is forming with alarming clarity.

"'Not fulfilling responsibilities.'"

"Yes. He skips school all the time."

"'Withdrawal from family and friends?'"

"Yes, I think so.... He used to be a real party guy, apparently. Always surrounded by a crowd. At least one girl, always a buddy or two. Everywhere he went was a party. But now... he's always alone."

Mr. H sighs.

"This one's important, Sarah Jo. 'A sudden and unexpected change to a cheerful attitude.' Did you notice that with him?" Mr. H's face is intent on mine, one hundred percent concentrated on my impressions. In spite of the content of our conversation,

I bask in his faith in me. Paul's easy manner comes to mind, his lightheartedness the night he left on his car trip. His carefree smile when he came to get me at Aunt Cassie's. No dark brooding eyes, that night.

"Yes, definitely," I say with conviction. "That's just how he was that night. He had always been so…distant with me. So cool. In fact, I didn't think I had even registered with him, really. And then all of a sudden he was at the door, asking for me. Perfectly cheerful and friendly. It seemed so—so weird. So wrong. It didn't fit with what he was doing. He gave back my scarf. He said he was leaving…just a car trip he said, no big deal. But he said all these nice things about me, told me how much my friendship meant to him. It was like he was—ending something. Like he didn't expect to see me again." A cold chill makes my spine wriggle.

"And I wasn't the only one who felt that. He said the same kind of things to my cousin, Madison. She got the impression he was kissing her off, in favour of me."

The horror of it, the simplicity of it, is dawning on me.

"Madison thought he was just being nice because he was breaking off with her to go out with me!" I laugh, a kind of hard cracking noise devoid of mirth. "I told her that wasn't it at all—and it wasn't. I just…knew…something tight in my stomach told me it would be the last time I saw him."

Mr. H nods.

"You are a very perceptive person, Sarah Joanne."

Now the words come spilling out of me like a great wave.

"In fact, Madison went up to the hospital to see him after we found out about the accident—he was flown by air ambulance to the hospital here. He had surgery on his knee, because when the car buckled…he went off the road and hit the ditch…he's so lucky he didn't die." My throat tightens. "They had to pry him out of the wreck, but he—I guess he was drunk, or high or something—he was asleep, they think, when he left the road, so his body was relaxed when he hit the ditch. He just kind of crumpled into the space under the dash." I shake the image off. "Anyway, Madison was up at the hospital last night, as soon as he arrived. The visitors' room was packed with his friends, she said: his buddies, old girlfriends, even a few teachers, they were all there. Everyone he used to hang with was there..."

Mr. H's voice inserts itself quietly.

"Why weren't you there, Sarah Jo?"

The question takes me unawares.

"Well, I..." I stammer, not really knowing the answer. "I don't really know him. I mean, we aren't really even friends. I've only ever talked to him a couple of times. And then there's Madison... I just... I guess I just thought I didn't belong. That I had no right to be there."

Mr. H smiles a warm encouraging grin, all the more comforting because of its homeliness.

"But it sounds like he confided in you. Maybe he knew you would listen. That you might understand?"

"The Mystic Cross link, you mean?"

Mr. H winces.

"By intuition?"

Mr. H shrugs. "Maybe he saw something in you that he *recognized.*"

My mind goes blank: I cannot imagine what Mr. H means.

"Please continue your story," he requests. "I think there's more, isn't there?"

It takes me a moment to resume the thread of what I had been saying.

"Oh yes. I was telling you how everyone, all of his friends were there, waiting their turns to see him. Well, Madison said they got to talking, and all of them—each and every one of them—had spoken to him the day he left, the day before his accident. He had telephoned, or dropped by. To tell them what good friends they were. How much he thought of them. Every one of them, Mr. H."

The fog in my mind is returning. What could all this mean?

"Why would he have done that, Mr. H?" Suddenly, a thought—a solid, convenient thought—presents itself to me. "Maybe he had some kind of premonition. He knew, maybe, that he was going to be in an accident. Or maybe he had a dream or something, and realized how much he relied on his friends. He just acted on it and told them how much they meant to him. That's got to be it."

I sit back in my chair, determinedly optimistic.

Mr. H makes his saddest pudding-face smile. He shakes his head, ever so softly.

"There's another possibility, Sarah Joanne," he says quietly, tentatively. A strange fear, the fear of recognizing an ugly truth, springs up into my belly.

"That list of behaviours I read to you: I got them from this pamphlet from our local Mental Health Association. I think you'll have to agree that it sure sounds like your friend Paul. It may very well explain your intuitions that something bad was going to happen. It explains everything you've thought without knowing why you felt it."

"What is it," I say, the words sticking like glue to my tongue.

Slowly Mr. Habbernashy lifts the pamphlet from his desk, so that I can read the title on the cover. SUICIDE, it says.

***

When I leave Mr. Habbernashy's office (which I do as abruptly as possible, leaving him worried and frustrated, calling after me down the long, echoing high school halls), I stay for a long time in the safety of the girl's washroom, wondering what to do. I am torn in two, as though a brilliant light has lasered my life into two distinct and separate choices: follow the rules, or follow my gut. Do I go to my classes, as I am supposed to do? Or do I follow my instincts and go to Paul.

Tremulously, I stop at my locker, gather my things, head out.

In the school foyer, I am detained at the exit by an over-zealous hall monitor.

"You can't leave," he says. "You can't just cut classes."

"Yes, she can," a male voice says. It is Mr. Habbernashy. "Go," he says. "I'm meeting with the principal, to figure out what to do," and I am out the door.

The long hike from my high school to the hospital—the same hospital that still holds my mother captive—gives me time to think. Unfortunately my thoughts refuse to get in line. They spin around one another: a brain tornado. What if I am over-reacting? What if Mr. H is wrong, and all Paul suffers from is a bad case of delinquency and poor judgement. How do you say to someone: *'so, are you suicidal?'*

Or what if I'm psychic? What if our shared Mystic Cross means I'm destined to save Paul?

I am tortured with glimpses of understanding, but these hints of clarity just tease me, bolting quickly into the quagmire of whirling images in my head.

In short, I don't know what I'm doing. Or why I'm doing it.

Crossing the rail yard poses some problems; now that I am off the sidewalks, my feet sink into freshly melting snow. It is late February, and the ground is convulsing with an acute case of early spring thaw. Snow melts into earth, earth melds with run-off water, until the whole is a mess of mud and slush. Like walking atop a live octopus, its suction cups erupting from the muck to latch onto its prey. My boot disappears in a well of earth, but I wrench it back, standing one-legged like a pelican.

I will not be sucked under.

At the hospital, I quickly determine Paul's whereabouts; I am comfortable now, with the working of this place. Spurred on by a dread that time is wasting, I do not take the stairs as I normally would, opting instead to use the waiting elevator.

I find Paul alone in a large private room with a breathtaking view of the lake. He is flat on his back, most of him wrapped in layers of gauze; he is drilling imaginary holes in the ceiling with his dark brooding eyes.

Entering a sick room is difficult at the best of times: it seems such an invasion of the patient's privacy. This—barging in not only to view a backside flimsily covered in a hospital gown, but to pry into a soul—this I am reluctant to do. An image materializes of me sticking a finger, a whole hand, into the centre of Paul, right into the fleshy, murky, personal world of Paul: I shake it off. Perhaps it's more like he is sinking in quicksand, and I, on the edge, can toss him a branch.

The first step into the hospital room requires all my might. I plunge forward like a bound man off a gangplank. Paul, his eyes still piercing the ceiling, says:

"Well, that took you a while."

His voice is not kind.

"What do you mean?" I ask. Is he mad because I didn't come to visit yesterday?

"I heard you waiting there by the door. Trying to get up the guts to come in?"

"Yeah," I admit.

Paul sighs with great annoyance.

"Well, at least you came in. Hardly anyone else did. Apparently most of my friends were here. Although no one actually came in to talk to me. Party was better in the visitors' room, I guess. Mom and Dad stopped by for a minute, though. Between meetings."

"Well," I say, "hospitals are kind of scary for most people." I remember my first trip here, to see Mom, how Joseph pressed into me as if medical monsters would jump from the walls and gobble us up.

Paul says nothing.

Hey man, you love me, remember? I want to joke. Instead I walk to the window, stare out at the park vista stretching out across the horizon. The solid crisp outline of my former home across the lake, stands like a cardboard cut-out against the sky.

"The ice shows no sign of melting yet," I say, hoping it will sound—I don't know—casual? Cheerful? Meaningful?

How do you do this?

Paul grunts something meant to show interest; instead his hatred bleeds through.

"Have I done something wrong," I say.

He looks at me, a stab of anger. His eyes are not so black now: the pupil stands small in the centre of each eye, the iris shining a soft golden brown in the sun from the window. He turns abruptly away again, eyes mining the ceiling tiles once more.

"No," he says, bitterness dripping over the edge of the word.

I am at a complete loss. Standing in the centre of the white, sterile room, I am surrounded by hard polished surfaces: floor tile, plaster walls, cold hard glass, steely metal trim. Paul is an island of life in the cold man-made room. He is roped like a steer to the ceiling, the bed.

"You're hurt," I note.

Paul shrugs.

"Not that bad, really. Broke my legs in a few places, shattered one knee. Got some metal in my forehead. That's about it."

He sounds disgusted with himself.

"Paul, I don't want you to hurt," I try, knowing it sounds lame.

He explodes, spitting and writhing in his bandages.

"I don't give a damn what you want! What anyone wants. Nobody ever bothers to ask me what I want. I'm the one lying here busted up. My mother—" he hisses his exasperation between clenched teeth. "You'd think I did this just to inconvenience her. To throw off her 'schedule.'"

His rage subsides as suddenly as it erupts.

"Well," he says under his breath. "Maybe I did."

The whisper hangs in the air like a ghost.

But, today, I am not so afraid of ghosts.

"Say it, Paul," I plead. "Just say it."

"Say what," he snorts, his eyes averted.

"Tell me what—what you're trying to do," I plead.

He turns his golden eyes upon me, prepared for a vicious fight. But this time, I am not fooled.

"Tell me," I say. "I'll listen. Mr. H taught me how."

A long pause passes before his words can find their freedom; his laboured breathing softens to a kind of wretched peace.

"Ok. You want to hear it? I want to die. I want to kill myself."

His voice is calm. Resigned. He means it.

An earthquake breaks in me, beginning with the slightest tremble and cresting in a torrent of tears.

Paul looks annoyed with my sobs, but his eyes grow soft.

"Don't cry," he says. "It's not like it would be any great loss."

I want to speak, to say the one thing that will change his mind; but I can't think of anything, let alone say it. Still searching and sniffling, I pray for the skies to open up, to tell me what to do. I wish I were psychic, like Aunt Cassie thinks.

A nurse arrives.

"Well now, what's all this?" she asks in a burst of clinical cheerfulness. "You needn't cry, sweetie. He's a bit broken, but nothing that won't mend." Touching my shoulder as she goes by, the nurse fiddles with Paul's bed, his bandages.

"Need to pee?" she asks in that business-like manner. Paul shakes his head no, his face flushing pink.

"Well then, I've done my bit. Checked on the patient. Let me know if you need anything. Enjoy your afternoon, kids." The nurse departs.

Paul is looking anguished now; I am still snivelling illogically by the window.

"I don't know what's wrong with me," Paul begins. "I have everything anyone could want. Lots of money, clothes. A big home on the lake. A pool table. My own car. My own boat. Access to the best of everything. I have lots of friends, a party every day. Girls. My parents even love me, I think. They're doing all that work for me."

His composure shows no sign of cracking.

"I don't know why I—why I can't just get up in the morning and be happy. I just feel so heavy, like I can't breathe. Like it's too much just to put one foot in front of the other. Nothing feels good anymore. Nothing. Everything I do is wrong."

Paul curls away from me, hiding his face as much as his medical encumbrances will allow.

"I just want it to be over," he says simply.

"Don't turn away from me, Paul." The authority in my voice surprises me. "That's what my mother does. I can't take that."

I move to the other side of the bed.

"Just talk to me. I don't care how awful it is. I'm sure not going to point out your mistakes. Dang, I don't even know which way is up myself."

Our eyes collide, locking in a strange, embarrassing dance.

"'Dang?'" he says, mocking me, a promise of laughter behind his gaze.

I groan.

"Geeky, right?" With head in hands I bemoan my stupidity.

"Good tactic," Paul says. "Get me to quit crying the blues by calling all the attention to yourself."

"Oh Paul, I'm sorry," I blurt, suddenly on my best behaviour. "This is not about me at all. It's about you."

Paul shrugs, a heavy, somehow happy shrug.

"Loser," he fires at me.

"Suicidal maniac," I fire back.

And then he laughs. Just a small dark hollow laugh, but a real one. The back of my throat tingles.

"I hope you don't decide to die again," I say too sweetly, but with feeling.

"Did I die once already? Dang! I thought I botched that up." Paul's shame threatens to envelop him once more.

"Yeah. What a f---up you are," I say, trying to be worldly; the swear word just sticks out awkwardly, sounding ridiculous. My comment has the opposite of the intended effect. Paul's features become drawn, serious. He looks me square in the face.

"Why does it matter to you, Swampy Jo?" he asks. "What am I to you? You don't really even know me. I haven't exactly been nice to you."

"You haven't exactly been mean to me," I retort. "It's all relative."

He snorts: "Some hero I am. But really, why does it matter to you if I live or die?" Paul's question is an honest one. This is worse than being naked. My stomach jumps into my throat.

"I don't know," I cringe. "Maybe I'm just proud of myself 'cause I figured out what was going on with you. I don't know. I just know you can't die. You can't just choose to check out."

"Oh yes you can," Paul assures me.

All the fight goes out of me.

"Yeah, I guess you can. I mean, people do. Still, surely to God there's another option?" I am on unsure territory here, but I plunge ahead anyway. "Paul, is there anything good about your life? Anything you like?"

His face is once more turned away, but I can see by the movements of his eyes that he is thinking, searching at least for some thread of hope. It takes a long time. Finally he says:

"I like working on puzzles with my Dad."

His voice has lost some of its flatness.

"Not crosswords—not thinking puzzles. Picture puzzles. I'm good with colour. I can pick out the slight variations in tone and shade. Makes me a good puzzle maker. Dad and I used to lay them out on the dining room table, and Mom would crab that we'd better get the damn puzzle done before her clients arrived for Sunday dinner."

A shudder disguised as a laugh escapes.

"I like puzzles," he finishes.

It seems wiser for me to stay quiet, to listen, which I do with every fibre of my being. I listen to his sighs, building one on the other, ever deeper, like a stairway deep into the guts of him.

Finally, tentatively, when it seems clear that Paul has run out of words, I say:

"Do you like your dad?"

Paul raises his hand to his eyes, digging his fingers deep into the sockets and pinching hard at the bridge of his nose. The room has caved in, the very air sucked out of it; the silence of a storm about to explode. He has forgotten how to breathe. Then all at once, his breath returns in a series of poorly muffled gulps and sniffs: Paul's cool resolve has dissolved. His pain and the grief choking his throat make it impossible for him to speak. Paul's reaction speaks for him: you don't fall apart at the mention of someone's name if that person means nothing to you.

That is one thing I know.

"Does your dad know... he's this important to you? Does he know you want to kill yourself?" I touch his hand.

Paul pulls it abruptly away, covers his mouth.

No, he shakes his head.

"Can I tell him?" I ask.

He does not shake his head no; instead his whole body quakes in a kind of confused seizure.

All I can do is wait.

"This is too big for you to handle alone, Paul. At least I know that much. You need help," I soothe.

No, he shakes his head. The rest of him trembles. His fingers still dig deep into his eye sockets, trying to stuff back whatever black demon is trying to come out.

"I can't just let you suffer, Paul. If you were bleeding I'd call an ambulance. This is like bleeding to death, Paul. I'll find your father, and I'll tell him."

I get up from the chair I've been sitting in, by the head of Paul's hospital bed, not really prepared to leave but feeling I have to move.

All at once, Paul slaps his hand down hard on mine, pulling my arm back behind me as I move away from the bed. The strength, the urgency of his grasp shock me.

"No!" he says, a strangled scream. His face is contorted in something like rage. Or panic, perhaps. I think of Sunday school lessons: *'And there will be wailing and gnashing of teeth.'*

"No," he begs. "Don't leave me."

So I stay.

Chapter Seven

These aren't the best circumstances in which to meet Paul's mother. When I explain to her what Paul's told me, as articulately as possible (given that she's a lawyer), Mrs. Holditch snaps.

"Paul," she says haughtily, her voice like ice, "will do anything to get attention."

But I can tell by the way her bottom lip trembles that she is embarrassed to have the awful truth spelled out to her by a perfect stranger in a lifeless hospital hallway.

It is early in the evening, though it seems days have passed since I arrived at the hospital this morning to speak to Paul. Lunch time has come and gone, then supper time; Paul has long since refused his tray of dinner, which now sits on a trolley in the hall, untouched. The meal is oddly precise: a perfect mound of mashed potatoes drizzled with milk-brown gravy, one braised boneless chicken breast cut into three equal strips, and a scattering of brightly hued cubes and balls pretending to be peas and carrots. The whole is covered by a plastic dome, reminiscent of the silver type royalty might use. In spite of the weird artificiality of the food, saliva beads in my mouth. Nonetheless, I deny my hunger: an established habit by now.

Mrs. Holditch does not enter Paul's hospital room to discuss what I've told her with her son. I find that surprising. Cruel even. After all, I have just informed her that her only child is suicidal, and all she can do is pace the floor, looking annoyed, listing Paul's weakest traits.

"He's always been so melodramatic," she hisses. "He's always been too sensitive."

Not 'so sensitive,' but 'too sensitive:' as though the degree of his sensitivity has made him unacceptable.

"Paul never could just get on with business. No matter what we get him, it's never enough. He just looks at us with those starving puppy eyes, as if we had just stolen his food bowl!"

I realize she feels the need to explain herself to me, to excuse her son's behaviour. She makes a good show of exasperation, really. But I can see that she is really just plain scared. That is why I wait until Paul's father arrives before leaving. I suspect she might lose her nerve, and decide to ignore the whole thing. If both Paul's parents know, then I figure the chances of them actually addressing the issue are doubled.

Paul's father, Mr. Holditch, arrives looking relaxed and cheerful. He takes my news differently: at once his easy efficient manner turns to rage.

"Who the hell are you to stick your nose in where it doesn't belong?" he attacks. "Who gave you this cockamamie idea anyway? There's nothing wrong with my boy. He had a car accident. That's all!"

"It's true," Mrs. Holditch inserts, still pacing. The way she avoids her husband's demanding stare speaks volumes: she believes me. "The boy told me the same thing." She has mistaken my gender, an unimportant detail that helps me feel comfortably anonymous. With renewed courage, I divulge further information.

"Paul likes doing puzzles with you," I tell Mr. Holditch.

"What?" he yells, clearly confused. Anger still blocks his grasp of the situation.

I know that Paul can hear us talking in the hall outside his unit. Sensing it is time for me to go, I stick my head in to his room.

"Bye Paul," I say. "Your folks are here."

And I smile, because in spite of his bandages, his gauntness, his misery, Paul looks so beautiful. I feel in that one moment that I have saved some rare bit of nature, the lone member of an endangered species. Paul's face is blotchy, his eyes puffy; he is twisting his inadequate hospital gown into hard spirals with his hands.

"I'll see you tomorrow," I promise.

"Okay," he mumbles.

He doesn't say thanks because he probably does not feel grateful. After all, this may be harder for him, facing a life that he wanted to escape. Still, I am pleased to see him so glum: it seems worlds better than the bitter resignation of this morning.

When I leave, walking down the long echoing hall, Paul's parents are still poised at the door to his room, as yet unable to enter. Shock has immobilized them.

To triple the odds of Paul receiving the help he needs, I stop by the nurses' station. Haltingly, I manage to muddle out the story. The nurse looks at me wide-eyed. She scribbles a note on his chart.

"That's Paul Holditch, the car accident? Well, that illuminates things, now doesn't it! I'll call his doctor right away. We'll have him looked at for depression. There are medicines that help with these things. Thank you for telling me—so often families ignore the signs, figuring a good talking-to and a night out at the movies will fix everything. But clinical depression is a bit trickier than that: it's a physical problem, an imbalance in the body and the brain. It needs to be treated, like any other illness. You're very wise to let me know. A real good buddy." The nurse punches me playfully on the arm.

Everyone thinks that I'm a boy: a real testosterone kind of day. But I don't care: for once I feel sure of myself. I savour the sweet taste of my own confidence.

Buoyed by the moment, I stop by my mother's room before heading home. Mom is still frozen in place. In a fit of affection, I take her hand in mine. Surprisingly, it is flexible, in a waxy way; her grip conforms easily to mine.

"I love you, Mom," I say with feeling. "I don't know what you're doing in there, or if you can even hear me. But I want you to know I love you, and if you can find your way back from wherever you are, that would be great. I need you. We need you, Joseph and I both. Maybe even dad needs you, to be your old self again. Aunt Cassie's been great, but she's not you.

"You've got to pick a side, Mom; either wake up or die. And I don't want you to die. Wake up, Mom, please. We can figure this out together. Please just wake up."

I would have cried to emphasize my point, if I had the energy.

I kiss Mom's cheek before I go.

By the time I make the walk to the basement apartment at

Aunt Cassie's, I am ready for bed. No exercises tonight...just sleep. I even forget to weigh myself.

It is such a relief.

***

My mom melts before the ice on the lake does. On the first day of March, a wet and breezy pre-spring day, a nurse calls Aunt Cassie to say that Mom sat up and asked for breakfast, but warns that we shouldn't overwhelm her. "Give her a day," we're told.

I celebrate with a walk in the park. The wind feels like cardio-pulmonary resuscitation: a breath of fresh life-giving oxygen forced into tired lungs.

I'll bet even Paul can breathe again.

Paul is at home now, having been discharged from the hospital, so I stop by his big home by the lake.

"Hullo?" his voice says through a speaker by the doorbell. "C'mon in. I'm in the great room."

"In the what?"

"The family room. It's big and open...just go straight when you come in. I'm at the back of the house."

Thankfully, Paul's parents are at work: I am not very eager to see them again, afraid they might want to shoot the messenger.

"My Mom's awake," I say with a lightheartedness I haven't felt all winter.

"Lucky her," he says with an edge of bitterness. But he doesn't really mean it, at least not wholeheartedly. He is testing out his new crutches. Both his legs are swaddled: one in a wide support sock about the knee, the other encased in plaster from ankle to hip. His hair is growing in around the stitches high on his forehead. Another line of stitches snakes from temple to eyelid, where plastic surgeons removed a shard of embedded metal. He is a beautiful Frankenstein monster. He smells of sickness, that weird chemical smell of too much sleep and extra hours of rebuilding somewhere deep inside.

"This is harder than it looks," he admits, hobbling about the furniture unsteadily.

"Well if you had at least one good leg..." I jab.

"The left one's not so bad, other than the knee. And the right one's not so bad, other than the bones." He grins and something inside me jumps, doing a back flip.

"I guess you'll be getting back to school soon," I say, with unusual vigour.

"Nag, nag, nag. No, I won't be back at school for awhile yet. I can't get around too well, as you might have noticed." Resting against the back of the sofa, he pokes me with the end of one crutch. Sweat is beading on his brow, his upper lip.

"I have a tutor coming in," Paul continues. "Mom and Dad made arrangements with the school. A guidance counsellor will be coming in to give me private lessons, four half days a week, then he'll pick up my homework on Fridays, and have it graded by my teachers. You know him, Mister Happy Basher."

"Mr. Habbernashy!" I blurt, spirits soaring. My heart practically jumps from my chest and prances about the room. Mr. H will make it all better. I just know he can help Paul with his learning problems. Help him find out what he enjoys, what he can do well.

"You'll like him," I say simply.

"Would you sit down," Paul demands. "Your fidgeting is making me nervous. And jealous." He has lowered himself with difficulty onto the sofa. He looks like a turtle stuck on his back.

I do try to sit still.

"What about the drugs?" I ask.

Paul looks at me with a smirk.

"Are you asking for some? 'Cause if you are… sorry, the store's closed for repairs."

"No, no," I laugh. "I mean your anti-depressant medication. How is it? Is it helping?"

He shrugs.

"It's just peachy, I suppose. I feel completely normal. It's very boring. No highs, no lows. No chance of either one, either. Strict instructions from the doc: no street drugs, no alcohol (which is a depressant, y'know). Very bad for me, says the good doctor. No cigarettes, even. Bones don't grow back together—knit, I think the word is—bones don't knit if you smoke. Except when you're sleeping. So I'm on nothing but air."

"You have a new doctor?" I inquire.

"Yeah," Paul affirms. "Two. One for my bones. One for my brains: my very own shrink. Pretty fancy, don't you think? Now I have everything a poor little rich boy ought to have."

In spite of his sarcasm, he looks pleased.

"Do you like him?"

Paul shrugs again.

"First of all, he's a she. And yeah, she's okay. I'm finding out I'm a very interesting guy. That's a well-kept secret in these parts. Bet I fooled you, didn't I?"

"Not for a second," I grin.

Paul basks in my admiration, like a cat in catnip.

"I might not be who you think I am," he confesses, very quietly so that I know he means it. "There are things about me that you don't know. That you wouldn't like."

The sudden darkness of his features tells me he is probably

right. But there are things about *me* that I don't know. Some hurts are so ugly, they are hard to look at. So who says you need to keep picking a scab?

"It's okay," I say. "I don't need to know everything. My Aunt Cassie says 'there's no need to parade your private parts in public.'"

Paul snorts, humourlessly. With effort, he pushes away the shadow that threatens to mask his features.

"So, how's your mom?" he asks.

"Awake!" I am practically singing.

"You told me that already. Give me more. Like when's she coming home?"

"Soon, is all Aunt Cassie will say." I know there will be more pain to come with Mom, but I hang onto today's happiness with a vengeance.

"Gotta go," I say. "I want to shower before I go see Mom."

Paul gasps.

"Did you say shower? You could have at least warned me before you broke the news. I'm in a very delicate state, you know. So, you're taking up washing as a hobby, are you?"

If I had been cool, I would have cursed him in that clever, vulgar way that pretty girls can pull off. But there are some things you have to accept about yourself.

"I'm not going to make it a daily thing, or anything. Don't hold your breath." I hope to have projected the right tone of smugness.

Paul puffs out his cheeks like a spoilt child refusing to breathe. All at once I want to kiss him—not a real boy/girl kiss, just a happy its-so-wonderful-that-you're-alive kiss.

Of course I don't. Instead I turn too quickly, bumping into the corner of a table as I head for the door. The table tips, spilling a large coloured image of a Japanese garden onto the floor, where it shatters into a million puzzle pieces.

Paul groans. He plants those wide, brown eyes on me.

"Sorry," I cringe. "I've busted your puzzle. I just knocked an oriental fountain into bits."

"Nice work, Sam."

"Sam? Who's Sam?"

"You're Sam," he says.

"I am?"

"Sam, you am," he says.

"Paul," I say, shaking my head, "I don't need another nickname."

Unruffled, Paul explains:

"The name 'Sam' suits you better than 'Swampy Jo,' or 'Sarah Joanne.' You're Sam. My bodyguard," he beams.

This distinction tickles me. Still, I object:

"Your parents will never know who I am if you call me that. They already think I'm a boy."

"All the more reason to continue calling you 'Sam.' What they don't know, can't hurt you."

"Pardon?" I ask, confused.

"Do people still say 'pardon?'" Paul says, almost to himself.

With a sigh, I bend down to set right the mess I've made. My fingers scramble to pick up the pieces, but each assembled slab I lift just disintegrates into more pieces in my hands. Paul pokes at the jig-saw fragments with the tip of one crutch.

"Forget it, Sam. No big deal. Just leave the pieces there. I'll get my Dad to help me put it back together tonight when he gets home from work."

There is something wonderful hidden in his voice. A whisper of hope.

"Okay then, I'll go," I say. Then, on impulse: "It's so good to see you better."

"Not fixed yet," he balks.

"But better." We exchange a look that makes me tingle.

"What am I gonna do with you, Sam? I've never been friends with a girl I didn't screw."

I shake my head. "You are so offensive."

"But really," Paul continues. "I've never even kissed you. Well, not really, anyway. I suppose we fumbled around a bit, but I don't know if that really counts..."

"Stop," I plead. Heat rises from my collar, setting my cheeks ablaze. "Let's just forget all that." I mean it too, more or less.

Paul looks at me kindly.

"Okay," he says. "You're still underage, anyway."

"Paul! That's enough! I'm leaving, before you corrupt my young mind." I head quickly for the door.

"No really, Sam! Don't go yet."

"My name is not 'Sam.'"

His brown eyes twinkle at me.

"Okay, okay," he says. "Just don't leave yet. I've never thanked you, for taking me seriously. For staying there with me all that day at the hospital, after my accident, when I needed someone...to just care that I was even alive. To notice. Most people are after me for what they can get. They don't call me 'Pockets' for nothing: everyone had their hand in my pockets. Some for drugs. Some for sex. Some for money, because money makes for a good party. But not you. You didn't want anything from me. Which is a good thing, because you haven't gotten anything either."

"You don't know that. Maybe I get a cheap thrill every time I look at you." The truth is, of course, not far off.

He laughs, not realizing that my heart swells just knowing he walks the earth.

"Anyway," he continues, "I don't really get why it matters to you that I didn't care if I lived or died. And the 'Sam' thing—don't worry, I know who you are: Sarah Joanne Bradley. I haven't forgotten. But you *have* been my bodyguard, when no one else noticed I was in danger. It's a compliment, my calling you 'Sam.' It's like a secret code word. It means 'thanks for giving a shit.'"

"Charming," I say.

"It's a kind of bond between us. Me, the damsel in distress (or the 'damned' in distress; it fits better) and you the knight in shining armour. Okay, maybe not-so-shiny armour. Still, it's something, what you did."

Despite his posturing, he looks sheepish, like I may at any moment laugh at him.

"The Mystic Cross," I say, pointing out the lines upon my palm. "How could I do anything different?" Once again, my attempt at humour falls flat; which is just as well, because to be honest, a part of me believes it to be true. I want to believe it.

"Whoa!" Paul teases. "Don't I have one of those, too? Yup. Mystic Cross. There it is, just where I left it. See?"

"Smarty pants." I can't help blushing.

So there we are, our palms together, celebrating our victory.

"Dang!" he says.

Really, he is too much for me. I feel light as the wind.

***

Back at Aunt Cassie's, Madison is primping for a date.

"Oh Mom," she is telling Aunt Cassie, "you'll just love this guy. He's blond, and so tall. He's a football player: his shoulders are as wide as a bus, and his tight butt in that football uniform—!" Madison growls with lust.

"Sounds wonderful," Aunt Cassie grins, but half-heartedly. "Have you lost interest in Paul then?"

"Pockets? Freak, Mom, haven't you heard? He's fried. Gone off the deep end. He's on medication, for cripes sake. Seeing a psychiatrist! The guy's lost his marbles. I like my guys sane, thanks." Disdain drips from Madison's carefully painted lips.

For once Aunt Cassie looks at Madison with palpable disappointment.

"It's not a character failing to get depressed, you know. Sometimes there are reasons. Life is hard for some people, Madison," Aunt Cassie says gently.

"Yeah, right! Pockets has a hard life, sitting like a king on a mountain of riches. I should have such a hard life!"

Aunt Cassie opens her mouth, but changes her mind.

"Hand me that hair clip, Mom," Madison chirps. "Well, I'm ready! See you in the morning!"

She is out the door in a flash, curls flying behind her like the tail of a kite.

An undefined sadness makes Aunt Cassie slump in a kitchen chair. She fiddles with a crumb on the table, lost in thought.

"Aunt Cassie?" I ask. "You okay?"

She smiles at me, her eyes still melancholy.

"Just thinking, Swampy Jo. Madison—well, she doesn't understand that the world isn't always so simple for everyone."

"Like for Paul, you mean. And for Mom."

She nods.

"Yes. Sometimes, people suffer for things that aren't their fault. Things that may not have had anything to do with them."

I'm not getting it. Aunt Cassie elaborates.

"Sometimes, it's not the person who has lived through a hardship that gets depressed. Sometimes, the hardship gets... kind of diffused, into the air almost, and settles on someone who is completely unsuspecting. A little like chicken pox."

"Chicken pox?" I ask. "Depression is like chicken pox?"

"Yes. Sometimes, maybe. Like a person who is exposed to the chicken pox virus, but doesn't actually become sick with the disease. Instead, that person carries chicken pox, and passes it on to other people who have no idea that they are coming into contact with the virus. The person who isn't sick is the one who's been exposed to the chicken pox virus; the person who gets sick has no idea there even was a chicken pox virus, and still, that person is the one who suffers the illness."

Now I am truly lost.

"What do you mean, Aunt Cassie? Are you telling me that Mom got sick because of what happened to someone else?"

For a moment, Aunt Cassie looks tortured. Her mouth moves open and shut soundlessly, like a fish gulping for air. Finally, with great resolve, she speaks.

"Sarah Joanne," she says, using my correct name: now I know I'm in for trouble. "I can't pretend to understand why your mother—or Paul, for that matter—is clinically depressed when the rest of us aren't. Same food, same water, same people, same events. Still, some people suffer while the rest of us don't. But what I do know about your mother, and our family, might explain some of it. It might explain about you and your father. It's like an invisible thread that runs right through our lives. A thread may not seem like much—just a fragile piece of string. But if it's pulled tight, a thread can cut."

I think of a horror movie I saw once, where a serial killer

murdered his victims by wrapping fishing line around their necks and pulling, until the thread sliced deep into their throats.

"There is a thread that runs through our family, and it starts with me," Aunt Cassie continues. "Me and my father. I've been thinking about what you said a few months ago, when I told you that your father left because your mother believed he had molested you. You felt sure when I told you that nothing like that had taken place. Of course you were only five when it all happened: you might easily have forgotten the whole incident, just pushed the unpleasantness from your mind.

"But then again...your mother might have been mistaken. She might have misunderstood. Over-reacted. In a way, she had been trained to over-react to the slightest hint of sexual abuse. You see, *my* dad molested *me*."

Aunt Cassie's voice does not even shake, although I do.

"I was eight years old at the time. I remember it very clearly. It's something I will never, ever, forget."

The line of Aunt Cassie's mouth is hard, grim.

"I told my mother once, then twice," Aunt Cassie continues. "The third time, she stopped and listened. Really listened. And she heard what I was saying. She told me I was right to tell her, that my dad was wrong for touching me like that, and she promised that it would never happen again. And it never did.

"I don't know what she said to my father. Maybe she threatened him, or humiliated him. But he never did come close to me again. And he never touched your mother either, who was three years younger than me. Mom saw to it that we were safe.

"My parents stayed together—there was never any talk of divorce. Possibly my mother thought the situation was best controlled if we kept a tight watch. But things definitely changed at our house: Mom ruled the house with an iron fist when it came to my dad. He never dared defy her. He stayed away most of the time, drinking with his buddies, or working. When he was home, Mom rallied around her daughters like a vicious tigress protecting her cubs. The only contact my father had with us came filtered through my mother. It was safer that way: she never took the slightest chance that my dad would abuse me again. We never talked about it, but there was a bond between my mother and me, a kind of conspiracy to keep the family protected—that meant protecting your mom from all of it. She was only little, just five years old. She never knew what had happened to me. She still doesn't know. There didn't seem to be any point in telling her: the abuse was over, the danger had passed. We thought—my mother and I—that it would frighten her for nothing. Besides, we were there to watch over her. You see, we were always on the alert for signs of something suspicious. Not just with my dad. With everyone. If your own father can abuse you, then a whole world full of strangers certainly can't be trusted.

"The problem is, in spite of our efforts to shield her, I think your mom was frightened anyway. You see, Sarah Jo, she lived the fear. Every day, it was there, a dangerous thread of fear that tied the three of us together. Your mom grew up afraid, without recognizing it as fear."

As Aunt Cassie spins her story, my head is spinning also.

"So, you see, it's not a far stretch to see how your Mom was poised for discovering sexual abuse around her. She had been taught, every minute of her life, how to spot it, how to avoid it. From the time she was five years old and on, her daily life was coloured by the possibility. She caught the virus of our fear.

"Now, it's also possible that maybe your dad did molest you. Your mom might have married him because she saw something in him that reminded her of her father. Your mother never knew he had abused me, so she never knew she should be wary of him, or of men like him—not consciously, anyway. Our father was a man she could tease with her cleverness, but never really get close to, because our mother was always there as bodyguard, protecting her from what might happen. She was taught not to trust the men she loved. Your mom may have repeated a pattern she saw in her own family, without realizing the dangers.

"Or she might have mistaken the innocent words of her five year old daughter, because it was an accusation that she had prepared her whole life to hear. I don't know. I do know that she believes your dad molested you. She did not hesitate a second when you said your dad had touched you during bath time. And I was with her, encouraging her, every step of the way."

The memory rushes through me once more: a rushed bath, when Mom is out of town, my Daddy scrubbing me too hard with a bar of soap in his bare hands, shuffling me off curtly to bed because baby Joseph is crying in his crib. Of my jealousy, monstrous in its intensity; how I plotted in my young heart to make Daddy sorry he had chosen Joseph over me.

I want so much to believe that is all there is.

"He was just washing me," I defend.

"Maybe, Sarah Jo," Aunt Cassie concedes. "Maybe you're right. I suppose the only one who really knows now is your dad." This fact seems to make Aunt Cassie very tired. It doesn't do much for me, either. Aunt Cassie plods on resolutely: always one to finish a hard job.

"So there is the problem in a nutshell, Sarah Jo. My past affects your mother's present and your future. A single sharp thread through all of us. I'm sorry for that, Sarah Jo."

"It's not your fault, Aunt Cassie," I answer.

Oddly, this information lifts a weight off me that I did not realize I was carrying. It explains dad's chilly manner with me. Being suspected of a dirty deed is almost like having committed it: either way, my dad is not going to win. It might seem easier to him to stay as far from me as possible.

It also explains that peculiar familiarity Aunt Cassie assumes exists between us—the shared mission of women protecting themselves against predatory fathers. Up until now, Aunt Cassie was convinced we share the same past.

Perhaps it also explains Aunt Cassie's approval of her daughter's sexual behaviour.

"Is that why you let Madison fool around like she does?" It is an indelicate question, badly put.

For a moment Aunt Cassie looks like she's been slapped.

"Yes, I suppose it is," she admits. "I don't want Madison to grow up feeling that sex is an attack. It's my way, I guess, of getting back at my father. He has ruined too many women's lives with his lack of self-control. He won't ruin Madison's life, if I can help it. I want her to see her own desires as a healthy expression of love."

The whisper of an abusive father, still taunting a family that has long wished him dead.

I know I'm overstepping the boundaries by offering my opinion, but I say the words anyway.

"Do you think being that casual with her body is a healthy expression of love?"

Aunt Cassie flinches. "Do you think maybe I've let Madison go too far?"

I shrug. "Boys aren't toys. Maybe sex isn't meant to be war, but it's not a game either. After all, we're talking about actual people here."

Aunt Cassie considers this.

"Good point," she says, a half smile playing at her lips. "You continually surprise me, Swampy Jo."

The return of my nickname signals the painful part of the conversation is over.

"By the way," she says, "it's a long time ago now that this all started for you—nine years ago since your family split up. But it's never too late to try to make things right. Secrets aren't always best if they're kept."

I've heard the whispers of those secrets for so long now, felt tensions that I did not understand. Parts of my life have been stolen by these ghosts murmuring secrets around us.

"Swampy Jo," Aunt Cassie finishes, "I'm sorry about all of it. About your mom. About your dad."

"Thanks," I say, relieved to have someone acknowledge my loss.

Nothing has changed, really. Mom is still crawling out of the hole of depression—or something worse. Dad is still keeping me at arms length. Joseph is still far from home, living on the other side of the moat that divides our family. Still, knowing that someone else sees it with me—the ugliness, the pain—makes it real. The ghosts, the whispers, the fearful things I've felt but could not put a finger on, are not a product of my timid imagination, after all. I have sensed the invisible, and now that the shadows have been brought into the light, we can begin, all of us, to erase them. And I am not alone anymore.

As an afterthought, I add:

"Aunt Cassie? I'm sorry about your dad, too."

***

Mom's winter hibernation is over. In her hospital bed she is sitting straight, and so is her hair. She doesn't bother to smooth it down. She does, however, smile at me—a sincere maternal grin.

"You came back," I say, as if she's been on a foreign holiday.

"You just needed to ask," she says.

"Do you mean you heard me?" I ask incredulously. "Were you really just waiting for someone to ask you to wake up?"

Mom shakes her head tiredly.

"No, Swampy Jo," she explains. "It wasn't quite that simple. I felt like I was clogged up, like I was stuck in quicksand up to my neck. I couldn't move. It was like exhaustion had gotten into my bones. Like I was being sucked away into a black hole where I could just barely hear and see the people around me." She shudders. "The doctors have tried to explain. I wrote some of it down. I knew I would never be able to remember all those long words. See, on that paper on the window ledge? Yes, that's the one. I thought I might look them up, to figure out what happened to me, once I'm home and well again."

The paper in my hand is scrawled with Mom's shaky handwriting. Words like: *acute reactive psychosis, schizophreniform disorder, catatonia* and *mutism*.

"What does all this mean?" I ask, a bit frightened.

"Well, I'm no psychiatrist," she says, giggling at the thought. "But I guess having lived through it gives me some kind of authority. I understand some of the words. 'Catatonic' means I was stuck in one position, although I could be moved into other positions and I would hold them too. That's called 'waxy flexibility.' They think that this kind of temporary paralysis is a way of slowing down what you see and hear and feel..."

"Here it says," I interrupt, reading from the page, "'to slow down incoming sensory stimuli.'"

"That's it," Mom says. "It's a way of escaping everything that's going on around you so that your brain can sort it all out. Then the 'mutism' part: that's easy. It means I couldn't talk."

"What about 'schizophreniform,' Mom? What does that mean? Is that the same as schizophrenic?" I have heard of that, which I thought was just another word for dangerously crazy.

"Not quite. 'Schizophrenia' is a kind of brain disease that causes you to hear voices and pull away from people, among other things. 'Schizophreni*form*' means that it looks like schizophrenia, but isn't. It's like a copy-cat schizophrenia. The best part is, it will probably never happen again." The relief on Mom's face is obvious.

"What about 'acute reactive psychosis?'" I press.

"That means it lasts less than six months, and is probably caused by a period of extreme mental and emotional stress."

We share a knowing groan between us, then laugh at our joint misery.

"So," I broach, ever so carefully, "are you better now?"

Mom nods, rocking back and forth with a kind of happy, perplexed look on her face. "Yeah, seems like I am," she says. "Apparently, I have every good factor on my side: I had a relatively normal childhood, I'm female (women recover from this kind of thing better, for some reason), the illness came on suddenly and there's no history of it in my family. My brain scan is normal. They say these things can go just as quickly as they came. I suppose it's nature's way of providing a kind of enforced rest: like a coma, only it's your mind and emotions that need the time to heal, instead of your body." This interpreted diagnosis seems to satisfy her. "Yes, Swampy Jo, I'm going to be alright. I'm physically weak, of course, from being in bed not moving for so long. And I've lost a lot of weight." She stretches the flimsy hospital gown away from her gaunt frame. "But I'll fix that up in no time. Speaking of which," she says, eyeing me, "you look awfully scrawny, Swampy Jo."

At first I can't tell if she speaks with admiration or alarm; the fact just seems to take her by surprise.

"Hasn't Aunt Cassie been feeding you?" she asks, concern mounting rapidly in her voice. "My God, girl, let me take a good look at you, under all those baggy clothes."

She grabs my sweatshirt and pulls the fabric tight around my torso.

"Swampy," she says, near tears. "My little Sarah Jo, you're like a skeleton."

A mix of anger and of shame pulls me away from her.

"It's not that bad, Mom," I mumble. "You're over-reacting."

Mom's eyes are wide and round.

"No, I'm not, Sarah Jo." Too often lately, I've heard my real name spoken, and what follows has rarely been good. "You're nothing but skin and bones."

Deftly, I duck the conversation.

"Okay," I say with forced cheer, "I'll fatten up, if you fatten up." Even the word 'fat' catches in my throat. But Mom has taken the bait.

"Okay, okay," she answers. "Can you bring in some of my clothes tomorrow morning, Swampy Jo? I look like a scarecrow in these." She's right: Mom looks all bony neck and flimsy arms, like a stick man you could break without effort. I realize for the first time that thinness is not always attractive. But I don't tell her that.

"I'm glad you're back, Mom," I say.

She grins and frowns simultaneously, oscillating between tears and laughter.

"Thanks, my baby," she says.

There is so much I want to ask, so much I want to say. I want to know where she's been, what she's seen. I want to tell her what has happened to me, to those around me. The words trip over each other in my mind, never managing the trek to my mouth. Mom takes the reins of the conversation.

"Your Aunt Cassie was by," she says, not looking at me. After months of not seeing her eyes, a panic courses through me and I quickly change places to find her gaze. Mom continues haltingly:

"Your Aunt Cassie says—she has a theory. She says you know about your dad—of course you know. She says that something—something ugly, happened with her and my dad."

A heavy sigh escapes, rattling her thin frame.

"Aunt Cassie says she thinks the two things go together: your dad molesting you," the word strangles her, "and my dad molesting her."

I rescue her from this painful disclosure.

"I don't remember dad... touching me," I stammer. "I don't remember him doing anything wrong, other than scrubbing me a little too hard. Joseph was crying, and dad just hurried me through my bath and plunked me in bed, so that he could rock Joseph to sleep. I remember thinking I hated him, that I was going to get Daddy into trouble for picking Joseph over me. That's all. I was five and I was jealous. That's all I can remember."

Mom's jaw works furiously as she grinds her teeth, ruminating over my words. I watch the anger drain out of her like steaming bath water down a drain.

"I suppose you could be right, Swampy Jo," she says calmly. "I don't really know what happened, because I wasn't there. But what you said, the way you said it... I felt so sure. But, I suppose I might have jumped to conclusions."

Her jaw works some more.

"But what if I was right, Swampy Jo? I can't ignore the possibility. You're my baby girl. It's my job to protect you. Even from your father, if that's what it takes."

There is no malice in Mom's voice, just determination. The ghosts of the horrible possibilities.

The full realization of what this means to my family creeps from my toes up through my belly, then up my spine until it seeps into my mind. There are no arguments left. The truth is that a wide chasm separates my parents, separates me from my dad. A grand canyon of maybes. Maybe he didn't.

But maybe he did.

It doesn't even matter anymore which maybe speaks the facts: the doubt itself makes healing the gash between us impossible.

"Okay," I say. "I understand."

Which is more or less the truth.

Chapter Eight

Mom has been home for almost two weeks now: thirteen days, to be exact.

Thirteen days. A bad luck omen, the number thirteen. At least that's what people always say. But I don't know that I agree. Not anymore. Perhaps thirteen is a lucky number for my family. I have always known we are a little odd.

For thirteen days, Mom has slept and slept, but in a regular, normal way: rolling around to adjust bedcovers, groaning, even snoring sometimes. Waking occasionally, from hunger. Aunt Cassie and I, between us, keep her fed. Joseph is still staying with my dad, so I have nothing more to do after school than check on Mom and make her sandwiches, or cereal, or whatever food she asks for in her alert periods.

Sometimes, I just stand at the door to our room and watch her sleep, noting the heavy creases on her face from sheet folds held too long in the same position against her skin.

At first I try spending the night in Joseph's bed, but I get up so frequently to check on Mom that finally I just bed down in our crowded room. I listen to the sounds of her slumber, the mumbled breaking-through of dreams, and then I can sleep.

It may not look that way, but I know in my heart that Mom is coming back to me.

On this thirteenth day, she does just that. Crawling out of bed on shaky legs, she smiles.

She smiles!

"What am I going to do now?" she asks Aunt Cassie, upstairs at her kitchen table. Between words Mom pops lusty red cherry tomatoes into her mouth, quickly diminishing the supply.

"You could go back to university in the fall."

"Maybe," Mom answers. "But summer is almost here. I've got to get a job. Earn some money, to pay for school. To pay for clothes. More books. Big, scary, university textbooks. And I have to pay you, Cass. You've fed my daughter all winter, and I haven't given you a cent. I haven't paid my rent in—what?—six months now?"

Another cherry tomato disappears into Mom's frown.

"Don't sweat it, sis," Aunt Cassie says, her back to us as she stands at the sink, washing up more cheerful cherry tomatoes. "Your husband—sorry, ex-husband—has covered all of that. And your child support payments are up-to-date on top of that, all in your account."

Aunt Cassie still keeps her back to us.

Mom pauses, a cherry tomato poised on her lips, making her mouth seem as round and red as a clown's. She is trying to swallow the information that dad has paid her rent, my expenses, cared for Joseph, and kept up support payments so that she now has a little nest egg of funds in the bank.

"Really!" she sputters.

She doesn't say *'I guess he mustn't be that bad, after all,'* though her eyes say it for her.

"So you have some options," Aunt Cassie says. "You've got enough in the bank to tide you over the summer, if you want to take some time off to recoup your health, before school starts. Or you can get a summer job, pay your expenses out of that, knowing that the cash in the bank will cover tuition costs and books for September. You've got the freedom to decide."

The world seems so clear to Aunt Cassie. But not to Mom.

"You know, Cass," Mom admits shyly, "I've never really told anyone this before, but do you know what I want? The one thing I've always really, in the depths of my soul, wanted?"

We wait, Aunt Cassie and I, for her to disclose her secret.

"I've always wanted…" Mom pauses, searching for words to convey an elusive, lifetime desire. "I've always wanted to be sure. To know that I was taking the right path. You know, in my heart. To be sure I was doing what I was meant to do. I have always wished I would hear the voice of God, so I knew I was doing the right thing. I want to have a vision."

Mom spreads her hands out beside her face, miming the emotion of awe.

"That's what I want. What I need, now. To have a vision."

She is saddened by the thought, or more probably by the sheer ridiculousness of the thought. Even I know it: people do not have visions.

Well, sane people don't.

In that one moment, I am struck by a terrifying possibility:

what if Mom *does* hear the voice of God? What if she *has* a vision? I've flipped through the medical books Aunt Cassie brought home from the library at Mom's request, the ones that explain about 'acute reactive psychosis' and 'catatonia.' I've read about schizophrenia and its offshoots, and now I know that schizophrenics hear voices. Schizophrenics see visions.

Please God, oh please, I pray to myself, gripped by sudden panic, *please don't ever give my mother a vision.*

"Well that's all very fine and good, to want to have a vision." Aunt Cassie is cool-headed. "Everyone wants to know if they're on the right track. Life is complicated. And we'd all like easy answers. We'd all like it spelled out for us. It would be great to have an angel come down to say: 'Hey you. I need you to buy your groceries at that place on the corner on a Tuesday evening so that you can meet the man that will hire you, or marry you, or save you from disaster.' Or whatever. Sure that would be easy. But that's not what it's like, not for most of us. We have to guess. Make a million little decisions every day, and take responsibility for where those decisions lead us. You've got to just keep trying. You've got to trust that your efforts will always end up with something good.

"Sis," Aunt Cassie continues, "you can't hide and hope that a vision will come to you. What you're doing to yourself is not making your life easier. Not eating right, spending all your time cleaning and painting and getting everything just so, not sleeping—these aren't helping you find your way. They're confusing you, putting you off balance. They're making it harder for you to know the smartest thing to do next. If you want to be able to see the best opportunity, then you've got to take care of yourself: get some fresh air, some exercise. Eat right, and get a good night's sleep. Every night, not just once in a while. Go out where there are people, and have some fun. Manage your money reasonably. Live a balanced life.

"After all," Aunt Cassie finishes, "you can't have a vision if you can't see straight."

Which makes me smile, and Mom too, once she gets over being told off.

"That should be my motto," Mom concedes. "'You can't have a vision if you can't see straight.' You have a way with words, Cass."

Then we laugh—really and actually laugh—right there at Aunt Cassie's kitchen table. All our ghosts, all the dirty secrets that have whispered around me all winter, evaporate with our laughter. It feels so good to laugh!

***

That is why, perhaps, I do not feel cornered when Madison hip-checks me in the high school hall, on my way to Mr. Habbernashy's office for our usual lunch-hour discussion.

"Sorry," I say, not really paying attention.

Madison sticks out her foot, and I all but nosedive into the floor tiles, one of my feet hitched around her ankle, the other buckling under the zigzag of my leg, books coming down first.

"What a pretty shoe," I say on the way down, noting the soft pink bow on her iridescent pearl slipper.

"Yeah, like you'd know pretty, Swampy." Her voice sounds even more nasal than usual, as if spit is collecting in all her mucous passages, in preparation for a mother of a hork. My hands are now trapped beneath my binder, which is being pressed hard into the floor by my crumpled upper body. The bare skin of my cheek, neck and upper arms sticks to the gritty flooring in hitching, heaving slaps as I thrust up and ahead, trying to free my arms. Like some kind of hideous walrus. My elbow is still glued to the painted concrete wall, where, I can see now, it has left a bloody skid mark on the wall.

"Loser," Madison says, in case it isn't obvious.

Someone snickers. Then a bunch of someones. My face is still near the wall, my body awkward and gargantuan around me, pointing in too many directions, full of too much bare skin pockmarked now with small stones from the flooring.

"You sure she's related to you?" someone bellows.

"The kid with the big head," someone else says. "She's part of your family, Madison?"

Snickers and snide comments descend on me like evil spirits, pressing my face closer to the wall.

"What'd I do?" I don't really say it, I just breathe it.

Madison sucks in the mucous building in her nasal passages. I look up, and can see right up her nose. For a moment, I imagine she's going to launch a wad on me, but instead she just smiles. She probably looks pretty from eye level, but from down here she's all chin and nostrils. Her breasts and ribs stand out almost equally above her bare navel, which I note for the first time is one of those outie kinds, all linked up to her belt with metal rings.

"We are not related." Madison smiles. "Swamp monster here is just some crap-fungus that crawled out of the nearest moat." She pokes me with one toe. "In fact, I'm not sure she's real. She may just be a figment of my imagination."

Madison isn't really addressing me. She's making a speech to her subjects.

"Um," I say, at my most articulate. My nose is starting to run and I try to wipe it, close to the wall so that no one sees. Pebbles, erupting like acne from my cheeks, sprinkle onto the floor tile with hard, flat pings.

"She's crying," someone whispers, and laughter follows, careening around me like a skeleton with wings.

"Clearly we're not made of the same stuff," Madison clucks above, elbows out, teeth pointy and glistening from my vantage point below.

"True," I mutter to the wall. "I'm not at all plastic."

It's not much of a come-back, and technically not true—Madison is silicon-free, as far as I know—but someone has to stand up for me. I'm nothing but a puddle here, nose in the dirt, crammed into the crack where hard floor meets hard wall.

Madison's face grows like a bad dream, until she's nose to nose with me, her skin-tight jeans strangling her knees, each one bent in an opposite direction in an ugly ballerina squat. Someone says something flattering about her butt, and she pauses in her descent to smile and bat her eyelashes. Micronanosecond flirting. Then she's *all* ugly.

"What'd I do?" I repeat, snivelling.

"You sicked my mom on me, that's what you did, Swampy Jo. She's getting into all my stuff now, asking questions, setting curfews. Crap, is what it is. All crap! That's all you create, Swampy Jo: crap. Crap is what you are. You're nothing but a dirty little turd on the bottom of my shoe, Swampy Jo, and you don't belong in my house. Sure, people feel sorry for you sometimes, but you and I both know you're nothing."

"Okay, so I'm nothing, Madison. What does it matter then what I said or didn't say to your mom. You think I have power? Sheesh." My nose is drooling self-pity onto my top lip now, and I do what I can to wipe it with the heel of my palm, but I'm too close to the wall, too trapped, still, under the weight of my torso.

My palm gets marooned up against the wall, palm up, glistening with snot.

I see it, I actually see the memory of that night at Aunt Cassie's kitchen table when we unveiled the sign of the Mystic Cross that Paul and I share, I see the black rage of it balloon in Madison's black pupils.

"You're worse than nothing, Swamp-puppy. You're a thief. You stole my boyfriend—although you're welcome to all the disease and dementia he's carrying, as far as I'm concerned. And no matter what kind of bullshit markings you have in your hand, Pockets will never—you get that: never!—sleep with you. No one will ever want you. You're just a shapeless blob of dust. You stole my boyfriend, you stole my mother. You ate my food, slept in my bed..."

"They're cousins and they're sharing a bed! Jeezus!"

Madison flicks a dirty look at the rabble surrounding us in the hall; I don't look up to check, but I can feel the number of onlookers growing, the air dwindling as each new body plugs a hole in the crowd.

"Not the bed I sleep in, dirtwads, just one of the beds I own..." Madison looks back at me, "by divine right as the owner of my house."

"Well, technically," I try, "the house belongs to your parents."

"What is theirs is mine, and what is mine is mine. Get it? You don't factor in at all. From now on you'll go where I tell you you can go. You'll keep your grubby little hands"—she pokes me with one long, sharpened nail, and someone in the crowd of someones around us pokes at me, too—"and your god-damned, god-forsaken, ugly-ass bloated filthy carcass out of my family and into the quagmire where you belong. You are nothing and nowhere is where you live. From now on, you can count on no more mister nice guy." And Madison stands up, towering over me, her pointed, clogged nose high and her eyes and mouth turned down on me, pointed too, stapling me to the ground.

"So this is your mister nice guy routine. Needs work," I say, wanting to be funny but hurting all over. I am hanging onto the concrete block wall like I might blend into the paint, into the cracks between the bricks.

Madison's eyes flare.

"You go, girl," says the crowd, who I've still not dared to look at. Their hostility hovers overhead like ghouls in a graveyard.

"Yeah, Madison," I say. "Please go."

I wish someone would laugh with me. So I could get up.

Hoots descend on all sides of me, bouncing off the concrete block wall as Madison's hatred grows above, and then suddenly the crowd's urgings twist into the harmless sounds of contrived casual banter.

"Now what's all this?" It's Mr. Habbernashy, and a bit of my heart oozes out the concrete-block cracks and back into my heaving chest. "What happened here?"

I don't have to look at him to know that Mr. H is frowning.

A hushed snicker. "Nuthin,'" someone offers. "Girl just tripped. Was funny," the kid laughs, and someone else seconds the motion.

"She tripped, did she?" Mr. H does not sound happy.

"Uh-huh," someone says, the sound already moving away. The air begins to move again as the crowd crumbles.

"Did someone help her to trip, perhaps?"

No one answers Mr. H.

"Did anyone think of helping her up?" Mr. H says. The hall is practically empty now, squeaking sneakers and clicking heels moving away into the distance.

"She's fine on her own," Madison says, pushing the words through her nose, standing her ground.

What I wouldn't do for that kind of confidence.

Mr. H and Madison look at each other, and I look at them over one shoulder. Mr. H is frowning, Madison is smiling sweetly. My chest heaves once, twice, three times, four.

"Break it up, then," Mr. H says, still looking at Madison. "Not helping's as bad as harming. Go on then. Back to classes. Back to lunch."

"Whatever," Madison drones.

"Exactly," Mr. H finishes, tapioca eyeballs looking as menacing as they can, which isn't very.

Madison tosses her hair and walks off, not looking back. A gaggle of goofballs opens like a doorway, closing around her like a hug, and they move as a clump toward the caf.

The rest of my heart crawls out of the cracks and into my chest cavity, badly bruised; my heart, that is.

"Sarah Joanne?" Mr. H is leaning over me, eyebrows high, mouth crumpled.

"I'm fine. Really," I shrug. "Just leaving a little DNA behind for posterity," I say, showcasing the blood mark on the wall and the tatters of my offending elbow. "Hey, Mr. H, have I introduced you to my cousin Madison? Madison's back, this is Mr. H; Mr. H, Madison's back."

"Oh my," he says.

"Hey, I've seen backs before, Mr. H. No problem. The upside of a back turned to you is at least the person's leaving."

Mr. H's crumpled mouth crumples more. I'm guessing this is a smile, of sorts.

"Shall we reconnoitre in my office," he asks.

"Reconnoitre away," I say.

"To reconnoitre is to 'engage in reconnaissance:' to survey enemy territory."

"Very apropos," I admit.

Mr. Habbernashy escorts me into his office, where I see one of my knees is bleeding, too.

"I thought my knee-skinning days were over," I say, placing the plastic bandages he gives me into place.

Mr. H's eyebrows and mouth crumple and bounce. "So," he says.

"Mmm-hmm," I say. Now that the bandages are in place, the pain under them pushing into the soft clean gauze, I want to cry. My whole self slides down inside the emptiness of me, to pool in my socks. "That wasn't so good," I manage.

"I imagine not," Mr. H begins. "Is there something that can be done? Were you threatened, or deliberately hurt?"

No, I shake my head. "Threatened only with aloneness, and what kind of threat is that when it's what I've got already?"

Mr. H scratches the back of his neck and grimaces. His discomfort runs on frantic feet around the walls of the room, making my own discomfort worse. I need to stop it.

"I just want to die," I say. It's a relief to finally get it out.

"Oh Sarah Jo," he says.

"No, not like that. Not on purpose, like that. I mean I want to disappear. I want it all to stop. I want to blend in and go away. I want it all to go away. In a way, I'm already dead. I don't really exist. My dad doesn't see me, my Mom can't see me, my little brother is far away. My home, the basement apartment at Aunt Cassie's, it isn't mine. It isn't anyone's. It's just really nicely painted empty rooms. I don't exist at all. I'm completely invisible."

"I'd say your cousin Madison certainly saw you, just now." Mr. H is looking angry. Not at me, maybe, but angry just the same. "I'd say she feels threatened by you. By how bright you are. By how loveable you are."

"No." I shake my head, which feels entirely devoid of feeling. All my sensations are trapped in the pulsing throbs of pain at my joints, in my sense of self pooling in the soles of my shoes, in a small hard pain in my chest. "Madison didn't see me at all, there. All she saw was the faceless people around me, laughing and poking at me. None of that was for me. It was all about her. I don't exist for her, except as a footrest upon which to dramatize."

My elbow and knee throb. How can scrapes hurt so much?

"Sarah Jo," Mr. H begins, "is this why you're starving yourself?"

All at once I am so tired. Tired and bleeding, with my self in my socks. Mr. H looks utterly lost. He rubs his face hard, as if there might be someone else with answers underneath his mask. But there's only crumpled Mr. H.

"What's it like, Sarah Jo?" he says. "What's it feel like, to be you? Maybe if I knew, if I understood... maybe... oh, try. Tell me. What's going on in there?" He looks at least as pained as I feel. His voice sounds very far away. My sense of self is in my socks, and pain prickles at my joints and in my chest, but some other part of me is hovering overhead, near the mismatched ceiling tiles, attached like a fragile balloon to the thinnest string of perception.

"It's like being inside a bubble of buzzing air," I begin, trying to explain. "Like there's distance between the outside of my skin and everyone else, like a fat electrified fence."

Mr. H nods, but he looks very confused. He squints and his ugly eyes nearly disappear.

"And there's the same bubble inside, keeping me far from my own skin. The only part of me that feels real is very small, and very hard. Like a hard-shelled pea."

"Like your body is too big to hold the real you. All air."

"Yes. Like there's this hard little pea-me..."

"Up in your head?"

"No," I say. "No, kind of in the middle of my chest, at the base of my throat. There's this hard little me-spot, and then there's all this buzzing, useless space between me and my bones and skin..." I can't keep the look of disgust off my face, "and then more buzzing, empty, impassable space outside of me too. So I'm very far away from everyone."

"Even far away from you." Mr. H is trying hard to understand.

"Yeah. My body feels too big, too soft. Insubstantial, like lumpy cottage cheese."

"Like you have no protection." Mr. H nods, as if he gets it.

"Right. Like the opposite of a suit of armour. It's just... flab."

"Hmm," Mr. H says.

"So there's just this pea, inside this lumpy cottage-cheese body that's no protection at all. And the only other thing I'm aware of, really, is saliva."

"Saliva?"

I nod. "Always. Saliva in my mouth. My mouth waters all the time, and the waterworks are tied to this little tangle of, well, pain I guess, like a barbed wire tangle in my stomach."

Mr. H clears his throat. "You're hungry."

I consider the idea for a moment. "Yeah," I admit.

"So why don't you eat," he asks.

"Well, eating doesn't help. It just makes the cottage-cheese body feel even softer and more useless. Not eating is the same as not wanting. It's a way of comforting myself. I feel more powerful if I don't eat."

Mr. H is shaking his head, fidgeting about as if his seat suddenly caught fire. "That doesn't make sense to me," he says.

"Have you ever wanted something you couldn't have, Mr. H?" He feels very far away, but if I zero in on his lumpy face, I can hold my concentration and his words get through the distance.

"Well, yes, of course I have. Not so much now, you get over these things you know, as you age. But, yes, when I was young, I often wanted things, sometimes very much, things that weren't practical, or were too expensive, or outside my skill set..."

"Okay. So you know what I mean. But if you can't have what you want, when you really have no hope of getting what you want or need, the best thing to do is not to want it."

Mr. H sits up straight, eyes blinking.

"And the more completely you can manage to not want the thing you want, then the better you feel."

It takes a minute for this to compute.

"So if you stop wanting something... stop wanting anything, then it doesn't hurt not to get it." Mr. H blinks, his eyes darting from one side of the room to the other, considering the possibilities in this.

"Right," I say.

"But you can have food," he says.

I shake my head in a small, restricted waver. "It's not about food. Not really. It's about not wanting. Because then not having feels okay. There's some power in it. Some choice."

"Ah!" he says. He rubs his face some more. "The opposite of self-comfort. Self denial, as a means of self-comfort. Don't want what you can't have."

"Um-hmm," I nod.

"Like not having enough love, maybe? Not getting enough care or attention?"

Oh, then new parts of me start to hurt. The wall of my chest, the band of muscles and bone that cover me, neck to hipbones, like a breast shield or a bullet-proof vest, tightens and expands at once in a solid front of pain. I won't let it out, though. I hold it there in front of me, buzzing behind it, and then I press it inside me where it quiets, and joins the small tangle of barbed wire pain in my belly, linked by a thin thread to the pool of saliva in my mouth and the hard nut of self-perception above my heart, at the base of my throat.

"It's okay," I say, calm as a monk. "I can manage. I know how to do this. I don't need much. I'm alright." It sounds like a mantra to me.

"Oh, Sarah Jo, oh my," Mr. H babbles. He's practically rubbing off his face. "What if someone loved you, loved you in a way you truly felt? Then what?"

I am so at peace now inside my lack-of-wanting that I feel I can try this idea on, slipping into it as if it were a physical thing. I imagine sitting in this room, right where I am, with Paul. Paul wanting to be with me; Paul laughing and looking at me, really looking at me. Paul reaching for my hand, the warmth of him spilling over into me…

The pain in my breast-plate returns.

…and then I imagine dad, holding me in his arms, him huge, me small. I see the white of his teeth as he laughs, smell the fine sweat at the back of his neck and taste the halo of cologne around his collar. I imagine the stubble of his hidden beard against my cheek and the heat of his lips on my forehead; hear the rumble of his voice saying 'my little Sarah Jo, my precious little Sarah Jo.' And then the pea-size me discards its hard, small shell and expands until I reach my skin and expand beyond it, encased in a fine, soft aura that has no wants, no needs, because all are satisfied.

"I'd feel safe," I say, and hurt pushes up from my chest through my throat and out my eyes in a silent, tortured waterfall. "If I felt someone loved me, then I'd know I was safe. That I served a purpose. That I deserved to exist."

Mr. H nods, his lips squirming about on his face, displacing his jowls. "Then you'd eat?"

I nod. "There'd be no reason not to eat."

Mr. H nods again. "What if you loved yourself like that?"

"But I'm nobody. How does having nobody love you count?"

"Is someone ever a nobody, if they love you?" Mr. H's voice is very gentle, distant and melting.

I think of Paul, all messed up and hopeless. His friends gone. His source of income gone. His pride in tatters. And I can't help smiling, which complicates my grief into some scrambled version of a laugh.

"Guess you've got a point there, Mr. H. I could try, I guess. I could treat myself like I was someone special." What a crazy thought! It makes me grin.

"Be your own best friend," Mr. H nods.

I shrug. "It's worth a try," I say, feeling marginally better. The hard pea inside me, the part I've identified as my only real existence, remains: unforgiving, insignificant. My sense of self is still in my socks, but I have a hunch that if I bent down, I could drag my pride and identity up to, say, knee height. And perhaps, with some practice, I might get the works up to navel level, like a pair of snug tights. I'm not sure I want to, yet. The lines in my palms, the Mystic Cross lines, are itching, all but humming. I clench my fists to hold them tight. "You never know. Self-love could work. I've always been a loner."

"Who better to start to get to know than yourself, then," Mr. H beams. "You're already so well acquainted."

The buzzing outside and inside my skin retreats a little, and the string-balloon of my perception overhead reconnects more fully with the me sitting in a chair in this dingy counselling office. A simple truth whispers through my mind. *What if I am the ghost I've been listening for: what if I am the secret I have yearned to discover?*

The smallest grain of hope, of pride, of wonder at myself and at a goodness I did not know existed in this world, springs to life. I unclench my fists, and my hands are heavy with freedom.

"Well," I say, feeling as though the sky has suddenly cleared. "This has all been somewhat illuminating, Mr. H."

In my mind I hear Paul's voice: 'People don't really use the word 'illuminating' in an actual sentence, do they?'

Then Mr. Habbernashy does something extraordinarily greasy. He gets out a package of peanuts, opened and half-eaten, and places the plastic pouch in the centre of his desk.

"So what's that," I say, eyeing the package like a terrorist. "A bribe? A test?"

Mr. H opens his hands, waves them around, moves his lips like a goldfish underwater. "They're nuts," he says.

"Obviously," I admit. Suspicion crowds into the jangle of emotion I'm feeling. "Am I supposed to eat them, and then live happily ever after?"

Mr. H waffles. "It's lunch time and you haven't eaten. I have, and this is what's left. I thought you might want them. You said you were hungry."

This is all so obvious. But my mouth does water.

"They're yours if you want them, Sarah Jo. I'd feel better if you ate. But I suppose in the end that's your choice." He is looking helpless again.

"I'll think about it," I say, but I leave the nuts where they are, in the middle of the desk.

Mr. H is looking sternly at me, forehead puckered, eyes

kind. "Sarah Jo, I am worried about your weight. Perhaps it's not the right time, but I do not feel it is wise to ignore the likelihood that you have an eating disorder. I've spoken to a friend, a psychiatrist (completely confidentially, of course, without naming any names) and I'm convinced now more than ever that you're anorexic."

Mr. H waits in case I balk, but I'm empty. Silence wraps around us. A fluorescent tube overhead farts a little electronic fizz.

"Please," says Mr. H, always the dutiful school counsellor, "see a qualified counsellor, Sarah Jo, for your eating disorder." He smiles his Winnie-the-Pooh smile, scrawls the name of a psychiatrist at the eating disorders clinic of our local hospital, then places the scrap of paper in my hand. "You deserve to be well, Sarah Jo."

I nod. Maybe, I think.

"Mr. H," I mumble, hesitating at the door. "Could you keep this between us, this psychiatrist thing? I mean, already the other kids think…"

"It'll be our secret, if you like, Sarah Jo."

Just one little secret, but I'm in charge this time.

"Thanks."

"Oh wait," he says. "Your nuts!"

"I'm not…"

"No, no. These nuts. They're yours." And he places the torn bag of peanuts in my hand, alongside the paper scrap with a psychiatrist's name.

I squeeze them hard in my fist, both forms of my salvation, as I go.

***

At my locker, I look at the opened package of nuts for a long time, salivating. I spill them into the cup of my hand. Salt into my Mystic Cross wounds. I consider making a religion of them: holding each peanut, tasting it reverently, sucking the salt off each separate moon, feeling the broken confetti of each nut descend down my throat into my gullet. After all, if Aunt Cassie can make a religion out of motherhood and if Mom can make a religion out of toilet scraping, then making a religion out of food doesn't seem so crazy.

Instead, I simply eat the peanuts, straight on, like the food they are. I pop a handful in my mouth. Chew. Swallow. Repeat.

There aren't enough to make my mouth stop watering. But about twenty minutes later, when I'm sitting in class, the distance between the world and me seems to shrink. The pea of me blossoms into a bush, new branches spreading out to touch the inside of my head, and the barbed-wire in my belly isn't so sharp. But my stomach rumbles, like an ogre being awakened.

On my walk home after school, I think: *I'll make a sandwich. Half a sandwich. Okay, maybe a whole sandwich.* I start to think about the non-hydrogenated margarine I'll use, the mustard (never mayo), the colour of the thinly-sliced chicken Aunt Cassie put in our fridge yesterday. I think of the blend of almost-yellow margarine with too-yellow mustard and barely pink chicken, seeing the resulting mottled-flesh colour. I imagine drooling, squishy blobs leaking out of the sandwich to stain flaking crusts of bread. I see the perspiration beads of toast-sweat on my plate, as my guilt and self-criticism bloat and my appetite retreats.

And then I stop myself. I stop my thoughts, full in their tracks, not moving an inch until I can turn away from the pictures, grown as big as drive-in theatre screens in my mind.

It's only food, I say. *Nothing special. (Nothing dangerous.) Not God. Not the Devil. Just food.* And then I think about something else, anything else—the cracks in the sidewalk under my feet, the sound of wind in the trees overhead, the calculus problems in my binder.

I think of Paul.

And the world comes closer to my skin than it's been in a long, long while. Time slows down and opens up. Smells, sights and sounds come out of hiding. Inner branches on my new, peanut-fed awareness, which has sprouted from a pea to a bush and now a hopeful tree, reach out to touch the long lost outside world, making friends through the bone of my skull.

Yeah, a sandwich, I say to myself, hurrying home.

Chapter Nine

I visit Paul at his house, often—as often as I can.

"You still talk funny," he says sarcastically. "No one in real life says words like 'ruminate' or 'nevertheless.'" But his words are playful, and they make me melt.

"Well, I do," I retort. "Now that you can read, you might learn a few words other than swears, yourself."

He throws a ball of socks at me.

"If you could walk, we could go down to the park," I say.

"Such cruelty, tainting me with what I can't do..."

"Taunting. I think you mean taunting."

He looks at me blankly.

"Rhymes with 'haunting,'" I say, "and means sort of the same thing."

He looks around for something soft to throw at me but comes up empty.

"Sockless, and hopeless," I coo.

"Yeah, well if you come closer I'll show you hopeless. And it won't be me, baby."

So I do, of course, get closer.

He looks at me, his dark eyes buzzing. Up close like this, when his pupils aren't bloated by some substance in his system, his irises are a warm, caramel brown, with little yellow flecks.

"You could kiss me, you know," I say. "I won't stop you." My voice is very soft. My heart is thumping loudly.

"I could," he says. The smile is leaking away from his face. "I shouldn't though." And he turns away, pokes at a pillow on the couch where he's marooned.

"Why not? I'm fifteen. I'm not that young. And you're only seventeen, just barely. We're not that far apart."

His eyebrows are working, but his eyes are on his hands which are manhandling the pillow in his lap.

"Is this because of Madison, then? She's dating someone else, you know, she's moved on..."

Paul snorts. The pillow in his hand is losing fringe at an alarming rate.

"I'm not jail bait. I'm not. And you like me. I know you do."

Paul's dark head of hair swings gently as he shakes his head.

"It's just that I ruin things. I go too far. I'm selfish that way." He looks tortured, and the pillow fringe is paying the price.

"Well then, stop."

He recoils as though I've hit him, but he laughs, and the last bit of fringe perishes. His caramel eyes dart to mine and away again. I can see he's not used to constructive suggestions.

"You can choose," I repeat.

"So, I can choose," he says defiantly. "And what about you? You just stomp your foot..."

"Stamp."

"...stamp your foot and say 'kiss me' and I'm supposed to pucker up?"

"Well, why not?" I'm on my feet now.

He squishes the pillow hard, strangles it, then tosses it aside like a dead thing.

"Sam. Sam. Don't go."

"I am not your Sam. I am Swamp...I am Sarah Joanne Bradley. I am me, for pissy sake."

Paul blinks. "You've got to work on your swearing, Sam."

"Yeah, well, your vocabulary sucks."

We glare at each other, panting.

"I know who you are. Sarah." He says my name softly, with reverence, as if the sound has never been held in anyone's mouth before. "Just...give me a minute, will ya? A guy's gotta get his head around this stuff, you know..."

"No, I don't know, *Pete,*" I spit. My shoes are already on. "Do you like that, when I call you some name that isn't yours? How recognized does that make you feel? It's just a kiss for pity's sake. It's not like it would be such a big deal for you. You've done this a hundred thousand times before."

The screen door clicks behind me, but not before I hear him whisper "Not like this."

And I want to go back, and I want him to suffer, too. I head for the park, leaving him bleating out my name, my real name—Sarah—into an empty doorway. While I walk, I wonder. Whether the Mystic Cross we share means anything or not, there is other evidence to consider. Our names, etched together on the black rock of the park, the ones I found one winter day:

why did Paul put them there? The snow is melted now, and the names pop up throughout the park, in the unlikeliest places, like eager spring tulips:

SWAMPY JOE
POKETS
(YOFUS)

I wonder why he added Joseph's name. I wonder what I mean to him.

I wonder if he loves me.

It feels so good.

***

And then Mom announces that we are moving again.

It seems impossible to hang on to who I am, without Mr. Habbernashy. Without Aunt Cassie. Without Paul.

"But Mom," I try. I want to beg, but I cannot catch my breath.

"Now Swampy." Her face is already turned away from me. "I know this is hard for you, but I've got to find my footing, and there's a job for me, in a new place. It's a fresh start…" She explains but none of it makes sense to me. All I know for sure is that it's all been decided.

"We're leaving two weeks before your school lets out, Swampy," Mom says. "So we've only got a few days to get ready for the move. I've cleared it with your school—you're such a good student, Swampy Jo, that I never get any trouble. Yofus will have to finish up his year in a new school; I know that's hard, Yofus, but it's only for a few weeks, and think of all the friends you'll meet. The drive will be a very, very long one. There's so much to do." She looks at me, her jawline drooping. "Now Swampy. Don't make this harder for me, please. Look at Yofus—he's even younger than you and he's taking this like a man. Come on, it'll be fun." But her voice doesn't sound fun. "At least you'll be free of Madison," she says quietly, as if this is our secret. Then she leaves me to my sorrow, with Joseph looking on, all wide, blinking eyes.

I cannot look at him. I look at the lines in my hands, my Mystic Cross, and I wish. I wish these lines could make everything right. Now. My heart, head and destiny lines intersect: red lines in a pink hand, like the scars left behind by a knife. Not hurting, like the rest of me.

***

"I wrote the names," Joseph admits. "The ones in the park. It was me."

We are lying on our living room floor, staring up at the high basement window borne up by the strength of an amber coloured wall. Pain is soaking through me, weighing me to the ground. I try to imagine the hurt draining out of me, through the concrete and into the earth. Willing myself to stay above ground until this barbed wired moment passes.

Sunshine licks at the mustard painted ceiling, in tongues of warm and cool light. I had not noticed before how dark it had been down here, with Mom gone. How long the strangulating shadows had crept across the ceiling. All I had to do to banish the dimness was to open the drapes, as Mom did when she returned home. Just open the drapes, and let the healing sunlight in.

It hadn't seemed an option.

"Every time someone walks in the park and reads our names, our story will be remembered," Joseph declares with confidence. "How you saved Pockets. Then Mom. Then me! Because otherwise, I could never have come home to you again." He says this with such enthusiasm that something gentle and warm tries to bubble up from my toes.

I lift my hand, and sun spills across my fingertips. Time hovers alongside dust mites in shafts of pure, clean sunlight, burrowing into our basement lair. Which makes my hurt expand and mutate, elation pushing a guttural form of shame up and out into the sunshine, too, if only I will let it.

I might just survive. Maybe. But I'm not sure I want to.

"But Yofus," I explain, "I found our names—mine and Paul's" (I can barely say his name)—"in the park in the dead of winter. And Madison said that the names were there practically from the beginning of the school year. If it was you who put them there, you must have done it in the fall, before the first snow. How did you know then that it would all work out?"

Joseph shrugs. An outline of his movement hovers in the sunshine, dust-veil disturbed, as if the motion were waves of pure sound. "I knew you liked Pockets when you first met him: I could see it. And he likes you too. He is always watching you. I could see that made you happy. And I heard, the night you said you had a magic sign in your palm. And that Pockets had it, too. Then, I hoped."

I take a moment to laugh inside myself, a bitter little cork, like a breath held. Pleasure and tension bottleneck in my chest, melding into a mélange that wounds and releases, like bursting bubbles of champagne.

"But nothing had gone wrong by then, doorknob," I accuse.

"Mom wasn't sick, Paul hadn't had an accident, and you hadn't gone to live with dad."

"You don't have to wait for things to be wrong before you wish for them to be more right," he coos.

"You sound like Aunt Cassie," I snort.

Joseph cannot be torn down. "I just knew something good was going to happen. Something that would make everything better. And it did. I got to live with Dad. Mom got better. It's a happy ending. So there."

His argument won, he settles back into the nest of his arms crooked behind his neck.

Fool, I think. I keep the thought to myself.

Joseph does not realize, of course, that our names all in a block like that cannot tell our story. He does not know that Madison and her band of halfwits will never know the truth of who put them there, or why. In the end, Joseph's graffiti will mean nothing to anyone but the two of us. But I do not ruin this for him. Because, you see, my baby brother is proud of me. And he doesn't know the whole embarrassing truth of it all: of incest in our family, of Mom's collapse and my anorexia. Of Paul, broken but healing. Soon to be far, far from me. The Mystic Cross we share has been no use at all.

The whole world seems ugly and hopeless.

Still, fragile shafts of sunlight flicker in through the basement window, shimmering. I turn my palm into them, and they illuminate the Mystic Cross. Like the quietest, gentlest hope.

"Kids, what do you think about periwinkle?" Mom asks from the other room. She is packing away our things again, mummifying them in crunchy brown-paper dressings. "It's a kind of purplish blue. I think we'll paint our new living room a periwinkle blue this time. No, please don't help, kids: I have my own way, it's less trouble if I do it myself. Don't worry, I'll pack everything. Nothing will get left behind, it never does. We take it all with us. You'll like the new place, you'll see. There's a deck to the backyard, and an apple tree. The blooms will be so pretty at this time of year. And it will be our own place, this time. Just for us. This time it will be great." She is rambling, comforting herself with the familiar rhythm of her own plans.

"Why did you put your name with mine and Paul's, in the park?" I ask, toying with this new pain, knowing it is immortalized on the cold, hard rock on the shores of a lake where I first saw Paul, windsurfing half-frozen in the cold September water. Near the hospital where Mom lay frozen in place for nearly six months. Across from the big house I once shared with my dad.

So many losses. So much I cannot take with me, and so much I can't leave behind. Each one of us alone, fighting our own private battles.

Joseph yawns, then proclaims:

"It's not every day the Mystic Cross changes lives."

"Yeah, yeah," I say, and I squeeze my hand shut around the miracle in my hand.

"I did it for you, Swampy. Because you're brave. And I put my name there because I belong with you," he says, "because you're fun."

"Give me a break, Yofus!"

"No really," he says, meaning it. "Who else would spend an afternoon looking at a ceiling with me? We go together, Swampy Jo. Everything's better with you here. Even as great as it was to be living with Dad, this is better. It doesn't feel like home without you." His voice sparkles with innocence.

So I accept my job, now, of packing away our secrets from him. For awhile, at least.

The light shifts, scattering new patterns on this moment's mustard-coloured canvas. In the next room, Mom sorts through our lives, cleaning things up, making it as right as she can. Crisp sheets of packing paper crackle in her hands, snapping like broken promises.

Another school. Another bedroom. Another futile flight to freedom.

After all, our ghosts go with us. They are part of who we are. At least now I know what we are trying to escape. And there are counter-weights. My little brother. The sun on a jewel-coloured wall. The adventure ahead.

"I'll always stick with you, Joseph," I say. "I promise."

He knows I will.

It makes it almost bearable. Almost funny.

Almost.

"Periwinkle will be good, don't you think?" Joseph asks. He bobs his leg up and down on the pivot of one knee.

"Periwinkle will be great," I agree.

The sunlight, shattered into shards, breaks over us in a waterfall of shining crystal tears.

***

My dad and I come as close as we can to discussing the rift between us, the day he comes to say goodbye.

"A walk in the park, Sarah Joanne?" dad asks me.

Mom's mouth is a hard line of disapproval.

"We'll come too," she says. "The fresh air will do us all good."

So we head out together but apart, two distinctive groups marching along the road, over the steel walk bridge, under the towering trees laden now with spring buds, to the park. My father and I walk silently in the lead, my mother, brother and aunt follow, chattering animatedly behind us, filling the awkwardness with words.

"Let's stay where Mom can see us," I concede, knowing she'll be watching, not wanting her to worry. The implied accusation takes the air out of him.

"I'm your father, for Pete's sake!" dad blurts angrily. I can see he is close to tears.

We walk through the park, which is as fresh and vulnerable as a new baby. Among the light and shadows, I imagine the ghost of Paul here, before he knew me, hiding somewhere behind these virgin leaves, indulging in pleasureless pleasures that have nothing to do with me. I wonder if he'll hide here again, once I'm gone.

The heels of dad's expensive shoes click cleanly against the interlocking stone walkways that cut the park into puzzle pieces. Dad cannot look at me. He points his face in my direction, but his eyes refuse to follow.

"I understand you're seeing a psychiatrist, Sarah Jo," he fumbles, fighting for control over his emotions. Anger is winning. It always does.

"Yes," I say simply.

"Is that really necessary?" he demands.

I shrug and nod at once.

"It helps," I say.

I wish he would crumple, would give way under the enormity of the loss of me. That he would sink onto a rock with his head in his hands to scatter his grief like healing rain upon the earth. For both of us, for all of us.

But his emotions never crest. They smoulder behind his

eyes, mocking me, making me feel that I am not worth the effort.

"Why did you invite me for a walk today, dad? Was there something you wanted to say? I mean, you've gone this long, barely seeing me. Why take me out for a walk now?"

Dad's mouth stiffens. He blows air through his nose like a bull, instead of answering.

"Am I embarrassing you by seeing a psychiatrist? Is that it, dad? Is that all you wanted? To ask me not to make you look bad? Well, we're leaving, you know. All my troubles and any embarrassment they might cause you will be far away, soon. So there's nothing for you to worry about."

Something is happening inside him, making him clench his fists, but he says nothing.

"I need you to like me, dad." I hurl the words like an attack.

His eyes retaliate. He looks at Mom, watching from a distance. And the chasm between us bloats, ugly and impassable.

The trees and lake breathe around us. The palms of my hands begin to itch. The lines in my hands—the mysterious criss-crossing marks that may or may not be real, that are my heart, my mind, and my destiny combined—begin to tingle. Then to burn. Then to hum in a frequency I feel rather than hear. Fragile new leaves on the trees shiver in this frequency, and the water of the lake that horseshoes around the park laps against the beach in response. With each pulse of wavelet against shore, the water grows murky. Thickens. Becomes sewage. Then burrows beneath the sand and grass and stone, snakes among hidden tree roots in the earth and explodes like a cola bottle under pressure, through the skin of parkland, into my dad. Fills his shoes and his limbs and his spine. Stains his belly and lungs from the inside, sprouting like hair-thin noodles through the sieve of his chest to soil his expensive shirt. Fills his head and ears and mouth and eyes with black, unforgiving soil.

And then the dirt becomes dust and falls away, as if the muck were never there.

It is odd to say, but the bitterness I've held against him, against myself, for his not loving me—for not loving us—drains out of me and away. He is punished enough for us both, for us all. With all that we have suffered, he has lost more than anyone. Whatever he is, a father or a monster, he is mine.

If I were to ask: 'Dad, did you do it? Did you molest me?' would I believe his answer? Perhaps you think it cowardly of me not to at least ask. But you are wrong if you believe it takes no courage to let a secret lie where it is buried. I have done all the grave digging I can take. For now.

This present moment is clear and I know all there is to know for now, standing nose to nose with my father's unbidden, impotent anger. I know he has no power. This is only pain. I know this in great detail. I know it in every vibrating molecule of my being. I know it in my quieting mind and marrow. I know it in my spleen and my digestive tract. In the diminishing buzzing in my forehead. In the decompressing birth-canals of my hair follicles. I know it in my stinging palms and prickling fingertips. In my fingernails, and in the flakes of dying skin beneath my finger nails, which are on their way to becoming dust, and in the new molecules growing in their place.

And so I finally bury the past.

Shake the dust off my feet.

I look up at the sun, at Mom and Aunt Cassie and Joseph in the distance, growing nearer with each stride. I let the filth fall away and in its place I choose something other than anger, other than despair. I choose life, and hope.

I let *my* story begin.

Right there, in the middle of my epiphany, Mr. Habbernashy jogs by.

Jogs.

With a lovely, shapely woman by his side.

"My wife," Mr. H introduces, pointing at her with his hands, with his whole body, as he runs. "Anna, this is the Bradley girl, Sarah Jo."

"Pleasure," the woman says. She is pink-cheeked and smiling, her nose and upper lip glistening.

"Mr. H!" I blurt, my mind once again boggled. The man I thought was a dumpy, slow moving school guidance counsellor is in fact a sturdy, thick-chested athlete with a charming well-rounded wife!

The pair jog by the immovable statues of my father and me.

"My dad, Mr. H... and Mrs., um, H."

Mr. Habbernashy turns around midstride, jogs backward for a moment, waves at my dad, and pivots again without missing a beat. Mrs. H lifts a hand and laughs.

"Knock me down," I say.

"Gym teacher?" dad asks.

I shake my head. "Fearless spirit guide."

I know I shouldn't be so surprised; that would be a kind of insult to Mr. H. But seeing them running by, both of them as solid as the earth itself, makes the world seem right and good in a way I cannot explain.

There is so much more to things than what I see. I may be intuitive and highly observant. But I am not perfect.

I am not perfect!

I say it over and over in my head, like a chant. *I am not perfect!*

And my release is nearly complete.

***

I sneak away from our basement apartment once the utility van Mom has rented is packed and she is busy with goodbyes to Aunt Cassie. Madison is away, on the arm of some blond thug in a dark daytime space, somewhere that is not here.

"Where you goin', Swampy?" Joseph looks worried.

"I'll just be gone a minute, Yofus. No biggie."

"Come back, quick," he says. "Don't wanta leave you behind or nuthin'."

"Uh huh. I'll be back."

The jog to the lake is quick, adrenalin beneath my feet.

Paul is there, waiting.

"You knew," I say.

He shrugs. Lifts his palm. "It itches."

He is leaning on one crutch, his body long and supple. His dark hair is in his eyes, the sun playing in its waves.

"I owe you something," he says.

I'm on him in seconds.

"Okay, okay," he gasps. "Breathing is good. And my balance, Sam, you're killing me…"

All it takes is a look from me to get him to correct himself.

"Sarah," he says. "Not Sam, I know. You're Sarah."

The name sounds kind, and strong, and new, the way he says it. *That's who I am,* I think, *Sarah is who I am.*

"Alright," I concede. "First we breathe. Then we kiss."

He nods.

And we do. Kiss.

The sun smells warm on his skin. The separateness of his

lips disappears into mine until where I begin and end extends into him. I feel as big as the park, as small as my hope.

"I can visit," he says.

I shake my head no. "We'll be too far."

He is painfully beautiful, dark and rich against the sun.

"But you'll come back." Not a question. For him it's truth.

"Um-hmm," I say, and kiss him again. My ribcage tightens around my bloating heart until I have to stop.

"Who will you be when I get back, Paul?" I need to know.

Paul pulls back and smiles at me. The padded corner of his crutch catches under my arm, and we topple together in a crooked dance.

"I haven't decided yet," he laughs. "What about you?"

I squeeze him, so hard he squeals and the crutch goes down.

"Anything could happen," I say.

A voice calls out from far away: a voice I know like my own. "Swampy! Mom says we gotta go!" It's Joseph.

We press our hands together, Paul and I, palm to palm, Mystic Cross to Mystic Cross, like a blood ceremony.

"I'll be back," I say.

He nods. "I know you will. I'll still be here."

***

So that's why our names colour the hard black rock of the city's biggest park. Our names are everywhere: on rocks, and walkways, on the bricks of retaining walls. But it is not Paul who puts them there, as I had once thought. It is Joseph's nine year old hand which writes

SWAMPY JOE
POKETS
(YOFUS)

again and again, in different spots that he feels are meaningful. He tattoos the park with our names, however badly they are spelt.

The tale of the markings in my hand, and the matching lines in Paul's hand, is now legendary in my family. Aunt Cassie recounts the story for Joseph, with some very elaborate embellishments, at the end of every phone call and after every Thanksgiving or Christmas or Easter visit.

"Yofus," Aunt Cassie says, "let me tell you a story, a magical story, about a brave girl and the lives she saved."

Aunt Cassie tells the story loud enough that I can hear it no matter where I am in our newest apartment: in the kitchen, in my bedroom, in the living room. Her voice carries, through the phone or across each room. I feel sure now, looking back on it, that Aunt Cassie spun the tale more for me than for Joseph. Her solid voice would conjure images of valour, courage, honour. Her telling of the tale transforms the memories, so that all the events seem somehow right, even preordained. Some people are very impressed by that kind of thing. People like Joseph.

People like me.

"Once upon a time," Aunt Cassie croons, "there lived a girl—just an ordinary girl. At least that's what everyone thought. She tried very hard to hide it, but this girl was special: she had the mark of the Mystic Cross in the palm of her hand. A very rare mark for a very rare heart. This mark joined her forever to a handsome young prince, who also bore the same mark. With courage and wisdom, the girl used her powers of perception—her psychic powers!—to save the kingdom. She knew Prince

Pockets was in mortal danger, when no one else knew it. The girl saved him when he fell from his mighty steed."

"How'd she do that, Aunt Cassie?" Joseph would interrupt. "How did she know the prince was going to have an accident?"

"They shared the sign of the Mystic Cross, that's how! The girl could read Prince Pocket's heart."

Joseph is always duly impressed, no matter how old he gets, even when I tell him that, actually, Mr. Habbernashy had a mental health pamphlet that helped, and the rest was easy. Well, maybe not easy. But clear, at least.

Joseph will have none of my logical explanations.

The fable persists in my family. When I feel unsure of myself (which happens quite often), I haul it out of my memory and dust it off, feeling the swell of naïve pride. I am a minor celebrity among my own blood relations.

"We will be remembered forever," Joseph says with admirable confidence. This is his way of making something beautiful out of our shared despair. The whole embarrassing truth of it all: of dad molesting me, or not; of Mom collapsing into catatonic hibernation; of Aunt Cassie reviving the ghosts of buried memories to help my Mom and me; of Paul wishing to die then having the strength to want to live. And of me, confronting my intent to whittle myself down to nothing so that I could disappear as if by magic.

All this is true, and not all truths are pretty. As Aunt Cassie says, the only thing worse than being caught in a lie is being caught in the truth. Yet all of the ugliness is erased, rewritten, transformed by my baby brother's refusal to see it. What has started out as sordid is rendered... miraculous!... by his simple faith. In me. Swampy Jo, the Mystic Cross warrior.

It is all too funny.